Mended
by
Moonlight

A Shenandoah Neighbors Novella

Also by Marsha Ward

That Tender Light
Gone for a Soldier
The Man from Shenandoah
Spinster's Folly
Ride to Raton
Trail of Storms

The Zion Trail

Mended by Moonlight

A Shenandoah Neighbors Novella

Marsha Ward

WestWard Books

PAYSON, ARIZONA

WestWard Books
P O Box 53
Payson, Arizona 85547
www.westwardbooks.com

Publisher's Note: This is a work of fiction. Names, characters, places, and incidents are a product of the author's imagination. Locales and public names are sometimes used for atmospheric purposes. Any resemblance to actual people, living or dead, or to businesses, companies, events, institutions, or locales is completely coincidental.

Cover Design by Linda Boulanger
www.telltalebookcovers.weebly.com
Book Layout © 2017 BookDesignTemplates.com

Mended by Moonlight / Marsha Ward -- 1st ed.
ISBN 978-1-947306-00-4

Dedicated to Sharon Oltz Kuhlman
a True Fan and True Friend

I acknowledge the help of my wonderful and gracious
Beta Readers: Laura Walker and Debra Erfert.
Thank you to those who allowed me to use family names
and other inventions for some of my characters: Loralee
Evans, Mark Kellner, Randee Dawn, and J'nae Spano.
Thank you to Dr. Fred Williams, my great-great-
grandfather. I honor his life and example.

CONTENTS

Chapter 1

"You needn't think to spend your entire life mourning for that Owen boy."

Ella Ruth Allen Owen sat on the old red upholstered chair in Momma's parlor that through the years had faded to brown. She hunched over the black-veiled bonnet that lay on her lap, gripping it between white fingers. Her mother's words buffeted her in their cruel unknowingness. Mourning for Ben was indeed what she planned to do until the day she died.

"I simply cannot allow it," Louisa Allen continued. "Black makes your skin appear terribly sallow."

Momma had ordered that the buggy be brought to the front door for the day's round of visits to Yankee women newly arrived in the South, visits that Ella Ruth found repugnant and intolerable. The vehicle hadn't arrived yet. Waiting always brought out Momma's temper.

Ella Ruth cringed as her mother continued to express her cutting opinion. *What does the color of my complexion matter? Ben is gone. Dead. I'd gladly join him if I could do so.* It hardly seemed possible that six months had passed since that dreadful day on which Roderick and Julia Owen had paid her a visit and given her the awful news. Ben dead at Waynesboro!

Stark grief welled up in her chest and brought with it pain and remembrance of those terrible first days of loss. Ben's parents had mourned, but she had been his wife. They would feel an easing of sorrow as the years went on. She never would.

Soon after she learned that Ben would never return to her, Poppa and Momma had come back to the ruined apple plantation near Mount Jackson where she had spent the last months of the war, and taken her to their now-preferred home in Charlottesville.

The place was foreign to her, even with a few familiar furnishings, like the old chair. It wasn't home. It wasn't her beloved Shenandoah Valley. It wasn't the nest she had built with Ben while she hid him and he recovered from wounds he'd received in a running battle with the Yankees. Her parents had left behind their old bed where, after an improvised wedding ceremony that consisted of her and Ben stepping across a broomstick as she helped him to the house—she finally had convinced him that the action was as binding as words spoken over them by a minister—Ben had elevated her from girl to woman.

She fingered the lump beneath her bodice, the slice of that broomstick that she wore suspended from a length of twine around her neck. It represented her wedding ring, her marriage certificate, her proof of widowhood.

Momma's sharp words continued. Ella Ruth wondered how long their argument would go on. A year? Five? All her life? Ben had been her husband. She was his, what was that ugly word? Relic. She was Ben's relic, and she would remain faithful to his memory.

The piercing throb started, as always, behind her

left eye. As the minutes passed under her mother's strident voice, she felt it envelop the space behind her brow, her eyes, her cheeks.

She put a hand to her forehead. "Momma, please stop. My head aches so. I cannot go with you today." With that, she got to her feet and stumbled out of the parlor, blinking back tears of rage and impotence.

When she was safely behind the door of the strange bedroom that she doubted would ever feel like home, she threw the bonnet to the floor and collapsed into tears on the bed.

She cried, beating her fist into the lump where her pillow lifted the sheet and the bedspread. Ben was gone, and never would hold her in his strong arms again. He never again would kiss away her tears, coax a smile from her with the brush of his knuckle across her chin, or make her laugh by telling her a silly joke. Never again could he make love to her. Never could he give her a child. She sobbed on.

After a long while, exhaustion brought a restive slumber, but when her maidservant entered through the dressing room door an hour later, humming a gospel hymn, she awakened and found herself still crumpled atop the bedspread.

"There, there, Missy," Lula said as she approached the bed.

Ella Ruth turned over, yawned, covered her mouth with her hand, and squinted at Lula.

"Your mama, she's gone off on her visits. Let me

turn down the covers and get you undressed, then I'll bring you a nice cold cloth for your head." She bent to pick up the bonnet, and took it to the armoire commanding one side of the room.

Ella Ruth pushed herself up to sit on the edge of the bed. "I'm sure Momma thinks it right for me to accompany her. I just cannot go. It's too soon."

"You had a bad, hard time. Maybe she don't know that yet."

Ella Ruth slid off the bed. "I haven't discussed it with her." She watched her erstwhile slave and continuing confidant pull down the covers and smooth the sheets, sheets that showed signs of wear. "She wouldn't understand. She and Poppa . . ." She touched the bit of wood dangling from her neck.

"Don't you be tellin' me tales on the master and the missus, now." Lula patted the pillow, and motioned to Ella Ruth to turn around. She helped her remove her dress and petticoats in silence, until Ella Ruth stood in her chemise, then she said, "You know I ain't supposed to gossip."

"I wasn't going to gossip," Ella Ruth said as she climbed into bed. "It's just that . . . Momma and Poppa didn't have a love match. They don't have any notion what it is to love someone so dearly and then—" She couldn't go on. Her eyes burned as though she'd been looking into a smoky fire. *Ben.* She didn't want to cry. She'd already done so quite thoroughly today.

She sniffled instead, and looked at Lula's dear, chocolate-brown face. Lula knew. Ella Ruth wanted to hug the woman, but that wasn't done, not even now that she wasn't a piece of property.

Lula's man, the one she had jumped the broomstick with when Ella Ruth was ten, had fallen from the loft of the barn five years afterward. He'd died a few hours later, wrapped in Lula's arms, rocked and hugged and sung to as he breathed his last. Ella Ruth had stood in the shadows of the apple grove and watched through the open window of the shack where Jubal died. Lula knew.

As Lula drew up the covers, Ella Ruth whispered, "Do you pine for Jubal?"

The woman drew back. "What you ask that for, Missy?"

"How long will this empty hole remain in my breast?" *Oh drat!* She felt her eyes filling.

Lula moaned softly, crossing her fisted hands over her own breast. She whispered, "It ain't filled in from then to now, Missy."

"That's what Momma doesn't understand." Ella Ruth sighed and blinked rapidly to forestall the fall of tears.

Lula turned away, saying, "I'll fetch you that cold cloth."

As her maid opened the door, Ella Ruth heard Lula's anguished sigh, and wished she hadn't brought up Jubal's name.

Momma didn't force Ella Ruth to go visiting the next day, but on the following Monday over breakfast, after her father left the table, the subject came up again.

"I've ordered the buggy for eleven o'clock, Ella Ruth.

You will be ready in the parlor at that time. I insist."

Instead of refusing, Ella Ruth sighed. The constant contest of wills left her stomach flighty enough that it threatened to bring up her toast and jam. *When will Momma see how much pain this tug-of-war brings me?*

"Yes, Momma. But you must promise to bring me home if I get a sick headache."

Momma arched a brow. "How long will this go on?"

"Probably forever," she whispered, already feeling queasy at the thought of being around her mother's new Yankee friends, expected to put on a cheerful face and forget Ben.

"What was that?"

"I cannot control the headaches."

"Perhaps you should see a physician."

"I don't know of any. This isn't my home."

"I believe the new hospital is almost finished. There will be well-trained physicians there after it has opened. I hear that will take place shortly."

Ella Ruth drew herself up straight. "It will be a convalescent hospital for those murdering Yankee soldiers."

Momma pursed her lips. "With qualified physicians, no matter their stripe."

"I don't understand why you and Poppa court those terrible people."

"Ella Ruth, 'those terrible people' won the conflict. We have no other choice, if your father is to resurrect his business." She paused. "If we are to live with a modicum of comfort, we must make these sacrifices."

Ella Ruth gritted her teeth. *I was never more happy*

than when Ben and I lived together, man and wife, without food, without luxuries, without comforts.

"You must do your part."

Ella Ruth carefully folded her napkin and stood. "The Yankees killed my husband."

"Blame General Custer if you must, but the Unpleasantness is over. The Federal Army won. We must make our peace with that."

"Do you care how it makes me feel, to make the rounds with you, visiting people who have come here as conquerors? It sickens me."

Momma's face softened as she rose. "I care that you are distressed, my dear. It wounds me to see you pining for that young man. However, life must be lived, Ella Ruth. One cannot withdraw from society." She moved toward the door into the vestibule and went through the opening.

Ella Ruth hastened to follow her. "I've done my best to do so."

Momma opened the door to the parlor and looked over her shoulder at Ella Ruth. "You're so thin, and so pale in those dreadful widow's weeds." She entered the room, which was swathed in soft, golden morning light that streamed through the open drapery. She sat on a horsehair sofa with a red fabric back and patted the seat beside her.

Ella Ruth preferred to stand. "I am a widow. I will continue my state of mourning." She clasped her hands together so hard that she winced at the pain.

"Daughter." Her mother drew out the two syllables until Ella Ruth thought the sound of them would shatter.

"You've mourned for six months. Surely you can start to lighten the colors in your wardrobe."

"If it had been Poppa who died, would you?"

"That is not the issue here," Momma said briskly. "The issue is that you are claiming a right I believe you do not possess." She lowered her chin and waved a dismissive hand. "Jumping the broomstick is a slave custom, and you are certainly not a slave!"

"Poppa always recognized such a marriage." She began to pace a path between her mother and the wall of windows.

"You are not a slave."

Ella Ruth came to a halt in front of the sofa. "I was a slave of circumstance. It was the only remedy."

Momma drew herself up to her utmost seated height. "I could understand a dalliance, in view of the circumstances, but no, you have to claim a marriage to the farmer boy."

Ella Ruth stood speechless. How could her mother say such a vile thing? She showed no comprehension of how important it had been to marry Ben, to prove that her long-delayed love for him was genuine, heart-felt. Didn't she understand how much better it had been to have a simple ceremony at that time, than to drown themselves in a carnal passion?

War had changed Ben, had made marriage and family important to him. If Ben had lived . . . if he had lived, they would now have been a family. At war's end they would have formalized their makeshift marriage with words blessed by a minister, renewed their vows under the beaming eyes of their parents.

If he had lived, surely their love would have borne fruit and she would now be carrying the child she so longed for. She laid her hand on her flat abdomen.

But Ben hadn't lived. Her girlhood dream of a big church ceremony had died long before he had. Her replacement dream of bearing Ben's child would never come to pass. She lowered her hand.

"I was fortunate to become his wife in the simplest of ways. I have a piece of that broomstick as my marriage certificate." *I have little more to remember him by.*

"You don't!"

Ella Ruth drew a breath as she sank onto the sofa. "Let us make a bargain. You will say no more of the validity of my marriage to Ben, and I will go with you to visit your Yankee acquaintances."

"Will you discard your mourning dress?"

She felt the fluttering of a throb of pain behind her eye. "Not at this time."

"I suppose I must be satisfied for now. Eleven o'clock, Ella Ruth."

"Eleven o'clock."

Ella Ruth sat in Mrs. Loralee Woolston's parlor, wondering if she was expected to say anything to the woman, or if Momma would carry the burden of the conversation.

So far, all she had been required to do was nod and attempt to smile, and drink sweet tea as she nibbled on a cookie. Then Mrs. Woolston turned her body slightly in

Ella Ruth's direction.

"Have you been widowed for long, my dear?"

Ella Ruth's hand began to shake and she hastened to set down her tea cup. "More than six months, ma'am."

The woman smiled brightly at her. "Oh. Isn't it about time you looked for another husband?"

The woman's words sent shock cascading through Ella Ruth's body until it left her numb. She attempted to subdue the anger that followed by drawing in a large volume of air. Then she answered slowly, "I do not feel haste is in order, ma'am."

"But six months! If you wait much longer, all the eligible men will be snapped up."

"Many of our men have died, ma'am," Ella Ruth pointed out, her back so stiff that pain radiated into her neck and shoulders.

"Oh, but I expect many a young man from the North to arrive presently, seeking a new place to make a start. My husband has several excellent properties to offer. Who else can afford to buy them?"

Although she tried to master it, Ella Ruth's outrage must have been apparent to her mother, for she quickly gave an answer.

"I'm sure my daughter will seek a husband when she is ready, Mrs. Woolston." She set down her own cup and saucer and brushed at her lap. "I thank you for the pleasant visit. We must be on our way." She rose and beckoned to Ella Ruth. "Come, my dear. We have other visits to make."

Departing as rapidly as she could, Ella Ruth waited on the stoop for her mother to bid Mrs. Woolston farewell, then accompanied her to the buggy.

"The nerve of that woman," Momma said, tossing her head with enough force to make the feathers on her hat dance.

Ella Ruth took her hand and pressed it. Momma had some sympathies for her after all.

Chapter 2

Alexander Marshall reined his horse to a halt before a large brick house on a dusty side street in Charlottesville, Virginia. The house looked tired and worn, fallen on hard times. That was no wonder. The owner had been a rebel during the late war.

Alex groaned a bit as he dismounted. His journey that day had been long and tiring, for both him and his mount. The bay nickered softly, hanging its head from weariness, and he gave its muzzle a pat. He looked around. He hoped there was a stable at the rear of the property. He hoped the owner had a trough of water and a bucket of oats for the horse. He hoped the owner had received his last letter with the bank draft intended to secure a room, for he had gone to much trouble to hire a cart to transport his household goods from Ohio. If the room had been let to someone else, all his trouble would have been in vain.

A boy came around the side of the house, a young boy wearing a tattered homespun shirt and linsey-woolsey trousers that ended above his ankles. His skin looked like it had been brushed with a dark tint made from boiled walnut hulls.

He can't still have slaves!

The boy had come near and stopped at a respectful distance. "You is Doctor Marshall?"

"I am." Alex let out a breath through pursed lips,

almost whistling in the process. If the boy knew of him, he must be expected. "And you are?"

The boy's eyes flitted from side to side. *He must not be used to being treated like a human being.* Alex let his question hang. At last the boy gathered his thoughts and whispered, "Horacio." He repeated it again, more firmly this time.

Alex nodded. "Well, Horacio, I see I am expected. Can you tend to my horse? Are there oats?"

The boy nodded back at him. "I tend to all the horses, Mister Doctor. We ain't got oats, but we have a little store of corn."

"That will have to do, Horacio. I'm obliged." Alex dug into a pocket and found a dime, which he pulled out and put in the boy's hand. "I'm obliged for your help," he repeated.

Horacio stared at the coin in his palm. After a while he put it into a pocket.

"I have a cart of small furniture and odds and ends coming, but it's at least a day behind me. You'll let me know when it arrives?"

Horacio looked up, his eyes alight. "Yassir, I will. You go along in the front door. Massa—Mister Lane will receive you there."

Changes take all forms, Alex thought as he unstrapped his kit from off the saddle. "You take good care of this horse, now. His name is Bugler. When he snorts, you'll know why."

The boy's face crinkled in delight. "Bugler. Yassir. We'll get along fine." He took the reins in one hand and let the horse mouth his other. "He's a tickler," he said, and laughed.

As Horacio led Bugler around the house to the yard in the rear, Alex arranged his saddlebags, a valise, and a bedroll into his hands and arms and set off for the door that faced the street under a porch that wrapped around the building. The door had once been painted white, but that had been several years in the past. Even with the shelter of the overhanging porch, it had weathered, enough so that bare wood peeked through the old paint in a few places.

Mister Lane and his family clearly had not had cash for upkeep of their property while the countryside rang with cannon fire and the clash of opposing armies.

The Marshall family hadn't exactly been abolitionists, but they did not agree with the idea that the enslavement of one man by another was just. When Alex received the assignment to return to the shattered South as a surgeon in a new hospital, he wondered how long he could stand living among a people with such different concepts. They were bound to be surly over their losses. How would his new landlord receive him?

As soon as he mounted the two steps leading onto the porch, the front door swung open. A large man balancing on a wooden crutch under his left arm eased himself into the doorway, wearing a suit of clothes that had seen better days. One leg of his tan-colored trousers was pinned up, leaving room for a stump that ended somewhere between his lower thigh and his upper calf. His face was bearded with ramshackle red hair that paired with lank auburn locks that hung to his shoulders. Blue eyes regarded him beneath brows that at first drew into almost one brow, then relaxed apart. Alex wondered if there was a loaded firearm within arm's reach.

"Mister Lane? I'm Alexander Marshall. Doctor Marshall. We've been corresponding." He put out his hand and the man met it with his.

"Obadiah Lane. Come in. I got your draft."

"I hope you had no problem with it." He followed the man into a broad hallway that hadn't been swept that morning.

Mr. Lane made a sound that could have expressed an opinion either way and continued into the parlor. He sat with difficulty, laying aside his crutch so it leaned against the side of his chair, and indicated that Alex was to sit, as well.

He found a faded green chair and perched on the edge.

"The C. and O. still isn't running," Mr. Lane grunted. "Did you hire a teamster?"

On his way into town, Alex had seen the ruin of the railway depot for the Chesapeake and Ohio line, alongside the beginnings of new construction. He nodded in answer to the question. "He should show up tomorrow or the next day."

"You'll have a bed tonight, such as it is. Horacio will help you bring in your furnishings when they arrive."

"He seems to be a helpful boy."

Mr. Lane leaned away, against the back of his chair. "He's sturdy." He stared for a while at the spot on the carpet where he would have worn a second shoe. "He gets wages when I have money to pay them." He cleared his throat. "Boarders help with that." He wiggled the toes on his right foot. Alex could almost see movements on the carpet from the phantom foot. "He's the only one I could keep on."

Alex restrained his toes from mimicking those of his host. He didn't know how to answer the man's comments on his changed fortunes. Finally, he shifted in his place and said, "I'm obliged for the room and board."

"Breakfast is at seven o'clock and supper is at six. You're on your own for dinner."

"That will do," he said as Mr. Lane struggled to get the crutch into place so he could get up from his chair. Alex slowly rose and waited.

Mr. Lane gave up the struggle. "Go on up the stairs," he said, waving toward the ceiling as he sank back into his seat. "Turn left at the top. Yours is the room at the corner on the left side. It has a fair view of the city."

"Thank you, Mister Lane. I'll see myself to the room." Even as he said it, Alex wished he hadn't. It was as much as pointing out the man's inability to show him to his lodging.

Obadiah Lane grunted and muttered, "Supper at six."

Alex gathered together his belongings and tried not to hurry from the parlor and up the stairs.

After a supper of corn pone, black-eyed peas, and some kind of boiled greens Mrs. Lane had named collards, Alex took his weary body to bed and slept fitfully, despite his exhaustion. He thought he dreamed, but when he awoke to a rooster's crow and budding rosy light, he didn't know if the woman in his dream had been Cassie or not.

Poor Cassie. Poor Alex. He'd been somewhere in Tennessee, sawing off bullet-shattered limbs and sewing up lesser wounds, when he'd received a letter from his mother that his fiancée had died of a fever. Knowing he no longer had a sweetheart at home, that he would not be marrying after all, had made it easy to accept a post at a hospital in the backwoods of Virginia.

The old twinges of guilt assailed him. If only he'd been at home, he might have saved her.

But he hadn't been at home. He'd taken his talents and training as a surgeon to war. How many years had he stood at his father's side and assisted him, learning which thickness of thread or cat gut to use on which body part? Which bone saw would do the job of cutting off a limb? Eleven. He'd been thirteen years of age when he'd begun his studies and training, and eleven years later, the medical corps of the Union Army had been eager to have him.

Father had practiced Dr. Fred Williams's Eclectic System of medicine and surgery, which he, in turn, had passed on to Alex. All the years of war had honed his skills, taught him plenty of shortcuts, given him a thirst for saving lives where he could, and letting men go on their way as gently as possible, if he couldn't. But he wasn't at home when he might have saved Cassie. That sore would gall him forever.

He was twenty-eight now, but he felt as though he were fifty, especially after attempting slumber on the misshapen mattress in this room, which had an upward curvature both from top to bottom and from side to side. The experience, he imagined, had been like reclining on an Egyptian camel's back. When his freight cart arrived, he would gladly exchange the landlord's mattress for the comfortable feather-filled mattress tick Mother had insisted he bring South.

"You must have a few comforts, Alex," she had said. "It's impossible to know if you can get enough feathers to fill a tick in that God-forsaken land."

He had accepted the luxury and stuffed it into the cart before he hightailed it out of town to avoid the memories he didn't want to resurrect. Women had no place in his life now. Why had he dreamed of one?

He swung his legs over the edge of the bed, and yawned as he got up to prepare for the day awaiting him. He would report to the director of the hospital, a Dr. Kellner, and learn what was expected of him. A surgical theater in a newly-built hospital would be a far cry from the field tents and barns he had become accustomed to using. Perhaps his dream was a portent that he would meet a woman or two at the hospital today. During the war, some ladies had devoted themselves to changing bandages and other services of charity. However, he did not anticipate any relationship with a woman. Certainly not a Southern woman. He would be kind, but he could not entertain his old fantasy of settling down with Cassie and growing old tending, to patients with the influenza, the grippe, mumps, measles, and other childhood diseases, and occasionally setting a bone or doing a surgery or two as he must. Cassie was a long-gone dream and he had become accustomed to living without her in his future. He'd better forget such vestiges of last night's dream as he might recall, and get on with his new life.

Alex found the hospital at the end of a long lane bordered by trees he might have seen in Tennessee, but didn't know for sure. They were nothing like the familiar Northern trees, such as ash and larch. He wondered if the director knew he was coming. Before he left Ohio, he had dispatched a letter with his travel plans, but mail delivery, he had been informed by his landlord at breakfast, was spotty at best.

A workman gave him directions to Dr. Kellner's office. A series of loud bangs came from the rear of the building. Someone still hammering on a project, he supposed. At the end of the main corridor, he turned at the last door on the right and rapped on it.

"Come." The voice rose over the banging sufficiently that he heard it, so he opened the door and entered.

The office was neat as a pin, reflecting the person who sat at the desk, a man wearing a dark suit complete with a light brown waistcoat, and a crisp, white shirt with a celluloid collar attached. He wore a cravat tied rather loosely below the collar, although he couldn't see much of it for the man's full beard. Alex noted the gold chain attached to a button of the waistcoat that disappeared beneath the unbuttoned outer coat, and hoped the man wouldn't consult the watch that surely hid in a pocket of the waistcoat. The man was occupied in writing in a ledger book with a steel pen. An open pot of ink stood on the desktop, the stopper laying nearby on a piece of blotting paper.

He approached the desk and removed his hat. "Doctor Kellner?"

The man carefully laid aside the pen and jumped to his feet, and foregoing any attempt to check the time, strode over to Alex and took his extended hand. He peered upward through eyeglasses pinched to the bridge of his nose. "Ah, it is Doctor Marshall, I think? Yes, I am Doctor Kellner, or as they call me, Director Kellner." His English was quite heavily accented with a foreign language Alex took to be French.

"Director." Alex nodded slightly as he retrieved his hand from the mauling grasp of the smaller man. "Alexander Marshall, at your service." He stepped back, not sure why he had added on the bit about being at the man's service. Perhaps he thought it sounded European and would be a proper greeting. It wasn't even his place to make the man feel at ease. That was the other man's job. Now he only felt foolish.

"Sit. Sit," the Director said with a flourish of both hands toward the straight chair standing in front of the desk. "Did you have a pleasant journey?"

"Tiring, but tolerable," Alex answered, sat on the edge of the chair, and balanced his hat on one knee. Dr. Kellner returned to his leather chair. His fidgeting fingers straightened items on the desktop as though he would rather be up and doing something other than desk work.

"You will like Charlottesville," said Dr. Kellner, examining Alex through his pince-nez eyeglasses. "You are not married?"

Alex shook his head. An odd question.

"The women are beautiful. Worn a bit by the war, but the young ones—" He stopped and put the fingertips of one hand before his lips and then appeared to kiss them, opening his hand suddenly into a starburst. "So delicate."

Not knowing what to offer in response, Alex remained silent.

Dr. Kellner left off his assessment of Southern womanhood as quickly as he had begun it and opened a drawer. He placed a few sheets of paper on the desk, and then turned them toward Alex. "You must sign to confirm that you have arrived and will accept your employment at the hospital," he said. "A sort of contract."

Alex felt his eyes widening.

"Yes, it is a document of my design, not from the medical office in Washington City. It states your duties and your desire to fulfill them. You will keep a copy and I will keep mine here."

Alex picked up the top paper to read. The terms and conditions it outlined appeared to be straightforward, but he'd never been required to sign such a paper before. Of course, he'd never worked beneath as tightly-wound an individual as Dr. Kellner before. The other sheet of paper was a copy of the first, so he took up the pen, dipped it, and signed both copies, keeping one for himself.

Dr. Kellner took the second signed copy, saw that he blotted it well, and then put it into his drawer. "So, now we will make the tour and see where you will work. Forgive the workmen about the hospital. They are going to be gone in a few days and we will be open for business." He turned and grabbed a top hat, which he placed upon his head with great exactness. "Now, onward!"

Alex followed him through the office door, bemused by the man's idiosyncrasies.

Dr. Kellner exited his office onto the corridor, and led Alex through three empty wards filled with empty beds clothed in white sheets and gray blankets, a pillow at the head of each.

Three wards, Alex thought. This is a large enterprise.

Then Dr. Kellner ushered him through two separate operatory suites. The medical corps had spared no expense, he saw. He picked up a gleaming new bone saw from a counter and ran his thumb over the teeth. What a luxury it would be to deal with patients in these surroundings. He put the saw back in its place and followed the energetic little director dancing away into another section of the hospital, which included storage and linen rooms, a laundry, and a kitchen.

The banging came from a workman assembling a series of wooden cabinets with hammer and nails, a good number of which he held in his mouth.

"You will observe the grounds to the rear," Dr.

Kellner said over the noise, gesturing through a window. "There is the space for a garden, a vegetable garden to be planted in spring. Our soldiers will have the best care and nourishment. Beyond there, you see the path of a brook, a little water stream for our needs. And there," he moved his hand slightly to indicate a small tidy building beyond the garden to the left, "is my domicile. Madam Kellner is entranced by the trees." He beamed as though he had conjured the trees himself especially to delight his wife.

"Very nice," Alex said, nodding at the amenities and comparing the cottage of the director with his own spare room. Of course the head of the hospital needed a lodging on the property. He had full responsibility for the lives of the men who would fill those beds, their lives and their deaths. Alex was merely a physician and surgeon attached to the institution.

The hammering ceased for a moment.

"The staff will arrive in the next few days," Dr. Kellner said. "Orderlies will be sent from the medical corps. Two ward matrons from Washington City are hired to oversee those who call themselves nurses, a few women to hold the soldier's hands in comfort and to change their bandages. I suppose someone has to carry out slops. We lack the third matron yet. I shall have to advertise in the newspaper for a suitable woman." He sniffed as though he thought women were unsuitable for hospital work, then scurried from the kitchen and headed down the dim hallway that connected to the main corridor. "You will have an office at the other end of the hospital," he said, allowing his hand to float in that direction. "If you come across a suitable matron, make haste to hire her. You have my permission. We must fill the post quickly. Quickly."

Alex thought it unlikely that he would be meeting women except as he passed them by on the streets. "I'll leave the hiring to you, sir."

The director sighed. "The women. Alas, we must have them in our lives to provide the comforts, but they do not have a place in medicine, eh?"

The idea that Alex would have a woman in his life now was another unlikely one. Cassie would have been the ideal wife for him, but alas, as the director had said. He shook off the dreary reality as he followed Dr. Kellner down the main hallway to view the two examination rooms.

"These are for the consultations on the best methods for curing our soldier's diseases," the Director said, then led Alex to the end of the long corridor and into the space that would become his office.

"There is the desk and the chair." Dr. Kellner's expansive arm gestures took in the furniture. "And here, the chair for the visitor."

"Should I expect visitors?"

"Some will come from the town: perhaps the mayor, the councilman, the Congressman from Washington City."

"The Congressman?" Alex had not expected that.

"Only if I am away from the hospital, you understand. Perhaps will come a person from the town seeking your advice on a medical matter. A physician."

"I see," Alex said. He didn't. He'd expected his work

would be on the wards and in the surgeries, not in his office entertaining visitors.

"That concludes the tour, Doctor Marshall. You are satisfied?"

Alex shifted his feet. "Of course," he agreed slowly. "The hospital is well appointed."

"I shall leave you to inspect your domain more closely," Dr. Kellner said. "Please arrive promptly at eight o'clock tomorrow. You may wish to arrange your surgery to suit yourself."

"Of course."

Dr. Kellner may not have heard his response, as he exited the room in his customary bustle of energy, leaving Alex alone in the room to open drawers and spin the swivel chair behind his desk.

Chapter 3

Momma quit making Ella Ruth attend every visit and every occasion to receive. She only insisted on including her in every other social event until two weeks had passed. Then one morning at breakfast she said, "I found a lovely material at the dressmaker's yesterday."

"Oh?" Ella Ruth felt a hand closing over her stomach. *What is Momma up to?*

"It's the most beautiful lawn fabric, sprigged with tiny white flowers. You will adore it, Ella Ruth."

"Lawn, Momma? Of what color?"

"Lavender. By spring, you will welcome new clothing."

"Not in lavender."

Momma helped herself to another biscuit. "It's a deep shade."

"People will think I don't mourn Ben if I modify my dress."

"It's customary to lighten the color of your apparel after a year."

"Momma, I can't do that."

"Why not?"

"I will be seen as caring less."

"You cannot persist in wearing black forever."

"Why not? I don't intend to marry again."

"How will you live, Ella Ruth? A woman must have a means of support. Your father will not live forever."

"Are you casting me out?"

Momma hesitated. "No. However, it distresses me to think of you wasting your life. You could marry, bear children, have a useful life."

Ella Ruth winced at the mention of children. Once, she had yearned for them. Now, it was not possible.

"Although I can scarcely abide the thought of casting you into the care of a Northern person, perhaps Loralee Woolston had an idea with some merit." She paused to gaze at Ella Ruth. "When spring comes, you must lighten the colors of your clothing."

"How can I bear to do that?"

"Women bear with a great many inconveniences in life, my dear. It is our lot, but also our greatest accomplishment."

Ella Ruth gritted her teeth for a moment, bracing herself for another contest of wills. "And if I don't?"

"I have discussed this with your father. He insists that you make a change in the springtime."

"You're placing the blame on Poppa?" *His will is stronger than Momma's.*

"It is his desire. He wants you to circulate in society. You cannot wear widow's black and do so."

Ella Ruth's heart turned over. Apparently her days of mourning had an ending point, at least in the eyes of her parents.

"I cannot betray Benjamin."

Momma sighed and spoke in a brittle voice. "He does not enter into your coming situation."

Ella Ruth held her breath. She thought her head would explode from the pounding within it. She put a careful hand to her forehead. She was to have one year then, one year only in which to remember and honor her few short weeks as Ben's wife. She exhaled, knowing the pain would not leave until she could get back to her bed and rest with a cold cloth brought by Lula. Only then would the pain recede.

"It will not be so dire as you imagine." Momma wiped her mouth with her napkin. "You may discover that you desire the company of other people beyond your family."

How could I? I'm no longer a dewy-eyed girl in need of chatter.

"You have room in your heart for more life."

Ella Ruth cast her eyes down at the scrap of ham rind left on her plate. *Never!*

Fortunately, Momma did not press Ella Ruth to accompany her on the day's visits, and she retired to her room. Lula had a cold cloth waiting and helped her to undress, and Ella Ruth sank into slumber, fending off the painful headache until she remembered no more.

Bye and bye she found herself struggling in the candle-lit parlor with a bolt of lavender cloth that unwrapped above her head, swirling her into its folds until she was caught tight, arms pinioned to her sides. She tried to fight, to wriggle out of the binding fabric, but it held her fast, until she fell in a heap and dissolved into tears.

She awoke then, screaming and thrashing against her encumbering bed clothing.

Lula bent over her, trying to soothe her with soft words as she tugged at the bedspread and sheet.

When she felt the bedclothes release her, Ella Ruth sat up, panting and whimpering, until her panic subsided.

"Missy, it was a bad dream, no more. You be fine soon."

"I'm not subject to nightmares," she protested, brushing her hair away from her face. Her muscles ached from struggling. Her head ach— No, it felt fuzzy, but did not ache at present. She slipped off the edge of the bed, wanting no more of it for now.

The cold air in the room raised goose flesh along her arms. She hastened to the fireplace and tried in vain to stir the dead embers to life.

"I'll get Thomas to build a fire, Missy," Lula said, and started to leave the room.

"Wait." Ella Ruth held up her hand. "Is it night? How long did I sleep?"

Lula turned in the doorway. "It be cloudy outside, Missy. You slept about a hour. Do you want a fire?"

Ella Ruth began to pace, rubbing her bare arms. She had to get out of this confining room. "No. Help me dress. I will take a walk in the garden to warm me."

"The garden pretty bare this time of year," Lula protested. "Nuthin' to see out there."

"Nevertheless, I need the air." She paused and looked at her servant. "Did Momma leave?"

"Yes, ma'am."

"You will say nothing of this . . . bad dream to anyone. Do you understand?"

MENDED BY MOONLIGHT · 31

Lula nodded, a baffled look on her face.

"No one. Tell me you understand."

"Yes, ma'am. Missy. I don't tell tales."

Ella Ruth sighed. "I know you don't." Her shoulders slumped. "I was so frightened, Lula."

"Yes, Missy, I know that." She went to the wardrobe and brought out warm clothing.

"Thank you, Lula."

Ella Ruth began to dress, bemused by the thought that she'd never expressed gratitude to any servant before today. Certainly never to a former slave.

Before she could exit the parlor into the garden, she heard a commotion in the hall, and Momma swept into the room, removing her hat and hurling it onto a table. "The nerve of that woman!"

Ella Ruth had heard that tone before, outside Mrs. Woolston's home, the day she had gone visiting there with Momma. She turned and looked at her mother, sinking onto the red sofa, her face set in hard lines.

"Is something amiss?"

"It's that Woolston woman. She has presumed to make a match for you."

"No. She hasn't the right." Ella Ruth rushed over and sat beside Momma.

"And that's what I told her, in no uncertain terms. She wants you to marry her son, who is studying at Harvard."

"A schoolboy? Quite absurd."

"He is reading for the law, and will set up his business here in Charlottesville this summer."

"You did dissuade her, Momma?"

"You won't be marrying her Yankee lawyer son." Momma's voice rang out in the room, strong and strident. "I told her that her meddling was quite unwelcome. I fear I must strike her off my list of friends."

Ella Ruth's stomach roiled. Would this disagreement spoil her father's chances of re-building his enterprises? Even though she had no intention of remarrying to aid in his plans, Momma's talk about Ella Ruth's need to secure a future for herself still echoed in the corridors of her mind. And yet, relief that Momma had fended off an unwelcome interference in their family affairs helped to quiet her anxiety to some great extent.

Forgetting her intention to walk in the garden, Ella Ruth spent the rest of the afternoon mollifying her mother's hot reaction to the "Yankee woman's" suggestions.

When evening came, Ella Ruth could not bear the thought of sitting with her family in the parlor, listening to her brother Merlin expound on what he had learned that day at the University. He'd taken a notion that he should become a philosopher. Poppa thought he should instead read law with a local attorney. They compromised when Merlin agreed to study history and mathematics, with an eye toward teaching.

Teaching! What has the world come to? She could not recall any Allen forebear who had been a teacher. Such a lowly occupation, instructing unruly children in their ABCs. Surely Merlin should bow to Poppa's will and become a lawyer. That was a prestigious calling. Or become a doctor, like Uncle Joseph.

Instead of taking her accustomed seat in the parlor after dinner, Ella Ruth hesitated in the doorway. *What can I do instead of sitting here and dying of boredom?* One glance out a window that had not yet had the drapes drawn told her. Moonlight lit the bare branches of the trees in the garden with white luminescence. The sight matched her condition: stark and barren. She remembered her delayed decision to wander in the garden.

"Momma, I believe I will take a turn about the garden tonight."

She retreated as swiftly as she could, despite her mother's protestation that it was too chilly, tossing a reply over her shoulder that she would wear her cloak.

At last robed in the supple woolen outer garment that Poppa had given her when winter came, she opened the gate and entered the silent refuge. A rustle among dead, fallen leaves in a far corner brought her to a sudden halt. A small animal escaped the debris and darted behind a tree trunk. She wondered what other manner of animal crept inside the garden by night.

When all was still once more, she set forth upon a path that had been swept of leaves during the day. Had it been Thomas who had done the chore, or another servant? They had many fewer sla— servants than in the past. Now there remained only Cook and Lula and Momma's maid and Thomas. Perhaps a day laborer had done the task. She'd seen freed slaves tapping on the kitchen door, seeking employment, if only for that day.

She wondered who hired day laborers. Did whoever answered the door take the man, or sometimes, woman, into Poppa's study to be interviewed? Did Thomas, the senior of their servants, act as agent for Poppa? Why did she even care? How servants were hired was no business of hers. They had always been a part of her life. There when needed. Especially when they had been slaves.

Now Poppa had to pay wages. How much did Lula earn to fix her hair and lay out her clothing, to starch and iron her bodices and chemises?

What was it Momma had said? Your father will not live forever. She shivered, suddenly cold, despite her warm cloak. If I do not marry again, who will provide for me when . . . when Poppa is no longer here? Dead. Like Ben.

The question sent chill fingers racing down her spine. Who, indeed. Who would take care of Momma's expenses? Pay the servants? Send the fees to the University so Merlin could study his inane classes in philosophy and history? *If something should happen to Poppa . . .*

Ella Ruth shook herself. Nothing will happen to Poppa. He is a strong man, sturdy as a walnut tree. He is not elderly. He will live for years and years.

And if he doesn't? If he doesn't? If some terrible accident should come to him?

She stopped, the hem of her cloak swirling closer to the animal's tree than she liked, but a melancholy mood enwrapped her soul and would not allow her to proceed farther along the path.

"Ben," she whispered. "What shall I do?" Her head

felt heavy, and her neck bent downward. No silver-tongued murmur came to her, assuring her of eternal devotion and watch-care. No husky whisper fell upon her ear, pledging a life of joy and contentment together. Ben's voice was silenced by war. She had no one.

Still she listened, and as she did so, she knew her attention was in vain. Ben could no longer speak. He would never speak again.

She sank onto the edge of the path, her throat swelling as she fought tears. Tears would do no good. She ought to know that by now. Months of weeping had brought no relief from grief and pain and loneliness. They would only leave her dry and barren and as lonely as before she began.

But the tears came regardless of her will, clogging her throat, threatening to make her nose drip in a most unladylike manner. *What do I care for ladylike behavior? There's no one to see me, or to care.*

She wiped her eyes on her sleeve and struggled to her feet. Her body had chilled. Her adventure in the garden had been for naught. Except it kept her from having to listen to an account of Cicero's or Plato's thoughts and theories. What did long-dead Grecians matter, anyway? What fascinated Merlin about the men?

Why did menfolk always get their say? She and Momma would never be allowed to discourse to Poppa and Merlin upon the delights of hosting a tea party or having dresses made or counting the silverware. Perhaps counting the silverware didn't, well, count. No one had any these days. Plain pewter cutlery and dinnerware had to serve at table now.

So many questions.

She felt a headache coming on, and gathered the cloak tightly around her so she could step quickly toward the gate and the kitchen door. She would go straight to bed, and forget Grecians and tea parties and death.

Chapter 4

When Ella Ruth's headaches did not abate, her mother sought a consultation for her with a doctor at the new hospital. A message from the director was delivered, saying that a physician named Marshall would attend Miss Ella Ruth the next day upon her arrival. Her mother delayed until breakfast the next morning to spring the appointment on her.

At the news, Ella Ruth inhaled sharply and dropped her fork. "Momma, you cannot think I would be presentable for an appointment this morning. It would take me hours to get myself together." In truth, she was already suitably attired for leaving the house, should it be necessary, but the awful thought of consulting with a doctor had not entered her mind as a plan for today. She picked up the fork and placed it across her plate, nudging it with a knuckle to improve the angle. "I don't want to go see a stranger, let alone a Yankee doctor."

"It will do you good to take a drive in the fresh air," Momma said.

"The cold air, you mean."

"Bracing air. You've been indoors too much, my dear."

Ella Ruth breathed in and breathed out, in and out, in and out, trying to calm herself in the face of her mother's unyielding attitude. Momma was going to win this round. The little quirk in her eyebrow told the tale.

Could she gain any ground, save herself any grief in exchange for her compliance with her mother's will?

Perhaps there was one pittance she could hope for. Ella Ruth took another breath and let most of it out very slowly before she responded. "All right. I'll go, if Thomas may drive me alone. There's no need for you to put yourself out to accompany me," she said, and went to get her heavy cloak without waiting for her mother's agreement.

During the buggy trip, Ella Ruth sat stiffly beside the elderly servant, glad for the lap robe that prevented him from seeing how tightly her hands were clasped together. *Where are my steady nerves? Did they leave me when Ben died?* So far today, her head had not tormented her. Since she was being forced to see a practitioner, she hoped the physician would conclude that if she were allowed to mourn in peace, the headaches would disappear.

When Thomas turned the horse into the drive to the hospital, she saw that a comfortable sum of money had been expended to construct the buildings. *Where did they get the money? Surely the Union is as bankrupt as we are from the expenses of the war.*

Thomas drove up to the largest building, halted the horse, and carefully alighted from the seat to help Ella Ruth down from the buggy. She told Thomas to stay with the horse, took a deep breath to steel herself, and walked through the front door.

Inside, light played on white walls of a small, empty vestibule. She pulled a bit of paper from her reticule and pushed through another door to encounter a hallway where a young man with no arm to fill his pinned-up left sleeve strolled past the door.

"Excuse me," she said, embarrassed to hear how timid her voice sounded.

The young man turned toward her and inclined his head slightly. "Yes, ma'am?"

"Might you inform me where Doctor . . ." She consulted the paper in her hand. "Where I might find Dr. Marshall?"

"Are you the new Matron?"

"Um, I— I have a consultation arranged with the doctor." She twisted the paper between her hands, disconcerted by the man's direct gaze.

"Ah. He'll be in the wards this time of day." He gestured toward a set of double doors on the right. "It would be more proper if you waited in his office. That's down the other way, the last door on the left."

"Thank you, you're most kind," she said to the first Yankee soldier she'd seen since Ben died. "I'll wait."

She turned away and fled down the corridor. She badly needed to sit, because her limbs threatened to give way from fright.

Dr. Alexander Marshall opened the door to his small office, thrust his fingers through the front of his straight black hair to tame a drooping lock, and stopped abruptly. A woman dressed in black clothing from tip to toe sat in the chair facing his untidy desk. She turned her head at the sound of his entrance. The customary heavy black mourning veil was attached to her bonnet, but she had already lifted it over the top of her head. The skin of her face was pale as the pallor of death, but her features were fashioned with exquisite symmetry. Pale blonde hair peeked out from under the black bonnet, and he drew in his breath, startled by the unexpected sight of such beauty in these dismal surroundings.

She was a young woman, scarcely old enough to put up her hair, although he could see signs of wartime privation in the hollows of her cheeks. He noted the lack of a companion, and wondered who she could be, come here so boldly, so alone.

He let go of the doorknob and nudged the door to swing shut behind him, enclosing the two of them together—alone—in his crowded office.

The woman had shifted the paperwork that had previously occupied the seat of the chair to the floor. He felt the annoyance, no, the embarrassment of having put her to undue labor because of his untidiness.

Suddenly aware that a bloody apron still covered his clothing, he removed it with haste, balled it up, and flung it into a corner. Then he dipped a hand into the pocket of his trousers and took out the unread note he'd received that morning from Dr. Kellner.

The only response from his guest came from her large blue eyes, which followed his every move. Otherwise, her rigid posture and tightly-clasped hands indicated uncertainty—or fear.

"Miss . . ." he began, then realized that since she wore the attire of a widow, he must address her differently. He glanced at the note. *Please attend to Mrs. Allen before noon. She suffers headaches.* "Mrs. Allen, I am Doctor Marshall." He dropped into the chair behind his desk and laid the note on the surface before him.

"I am Mrs. Benjamin Owen," the widow said, her voice firmer than he had supposed it would be.

"I beg your pardon," he answered, looking at the note again.

"My mother, Mrs. Theodore Allen, arranged for this visit. I am Mrs. Owen." Again, her voice conveyed her statement with firmness.

He inclined his head. "Mrs. Owen. How may I be of service?"

His question seemed to annoy her, as her brow furrowed. No, perhaps her expression was confusion.

Alex straightened his shoulders. He'd never had such difficulty reading a patient before this. But then, he'd never before had an entrancing young woman sitting across from him in such a small, stifling place. He wished he'd put on his coat, which hung from a coat tree positioned behind his desk. He shifted in his seat, aware that his collar had grown tight. He was accustomed to the company of men, patients whose arms or legs needed to be removed, men who had been injured in battle. Clearly, the woman was out of place in this military hospital built for the convalescence of Union soldiers injured in the past conflict. He cleared his throat, waiting for the woman to answer.

Silence rested heavily in the room, heavy as a blanket of wool. It settled upon his ears until he could hear the rapid beat of his heart. He thought he detected the rush of blood through his arteries. He hadn't felt this way in years, not since Cas—

"My mother—" she broke the stillness and stopped. She straightened her spine and began again. "My mother is concerned for my health."

"Are you suffering from some malady?" *She looks healthy enough. Aside from her pallor, I don't see any indication of illness.*

She touched her forehead briefly. "Headaches come upon me. Severe headaches."

Alex relaxed. Headaches he could deal with. A powder, a potion, perhaps a patent medicine. "Are they regular? Every day?"

Mrs. Owen shook her head.

He sat back in his seat, wishing for a cigar. It would give his hand something to do besides move the note around on the desktop. He badly needed to cross his legs, or jump to his feet and stride about the room. But the office was too cluttered for such freedom. He leaned forward.

"Have you found relief in any way?"

"My servant brings me a cold cloth, and I sleep until the pain fades."

The fingers of one hand twitched in her lap.

"Have you tried any medicines?"

She looked up, her eyes meeting his. "Medicines?"

"A headache powder?"

She shook her head, furrowing her brows once more. "Only the cold cloths."

"When does the pain appear? Are you engaged in activity or at rest when they come upon you?"

The woman seemed to consider his questions. Then she blurted, "When Momma is so insistent—" She stopped and drew a hasty breath, as though she had voiced an uncomfortable thought. "Oh."

"Do you and your mother quarrel frequently?"

She nodded, looking at her hands.

"Always upon the same topic?"

She nodded again.

"And what is that?"

Her torso stiffened again. She gave no reply.

After a long moment, Alex prompted her to respond. "Mrs. Owen?"

She touched a place on her bodice below her throat that he saw covered a small lump. Perhaps a wedding ring? "She wishes me to give up my mourning clothing to make a pretty appearance when I accompany her on visits."

Stunned at the bitterness in her answer, he waited for a moment, then asked, "Has a year passed?" Had her husband been a rebel soldier? Gall came into his mouth, and he swallowed it down with difficulty.

"No." The word was sharp and crisp. "I will not marry again. My mother cannot understand that I am opposed to reentering society, especially that of Yank—" She stopped, and her hand rose to cover her mouth.

His stomach lurched to realize that she saw him as the enemy. "I am a physician," he said as gently as he could, considering the turmoil in his abdomen. "I am used to hearing—and keeping—the secrets of my patients." *But not of lovely young women.* "You may speak freely. I will not divulge what I hear to another soul."

She took a deep breath and her shoulders relaxed.

"Are you distressed at this time?" he asked.

"A bit," she conceded.

"Am I the cause of your distress?"

"I am used to the company of physicians."

"Oh?" Had she some root illness for which she sought regular medical advice? No. That couldn't be, or she would never have come here. "How is that?"

She looked at him, her gaze direct. "I worked at the hospital in Mount Jackson with my uncle, Doctor Joseph Allen. He is a noted surgeon."

"You comforted the sick and the wounded?"

She rolled her eyes and looked down at her hands. He detected a tightening of her jaw. At length, she raised her chin and said, "I assisted him in surgery."

If she had socked him in the stomach, he could not have been more surprised. He leaned forward. "You what?"

She sighed and raised one shoulder. "It was necessary, and most useful training to me."

"Your husband allowed—"

"I was unmarried at the time. We all did our part." She pursed her lips, then spoke again. "I performed surgery on him."

"Who?" He hoped his face didn't reflect his disbelief.

"My husband," she whispered.

He leaned back. And undoubtedly caused his death.

"He was cured," she said, her voice sharp, as though she had noted his incredulity. "He died in battle afterward. At Waynesboro."

Waynesboro. One of the last battles.

"I shall not remarry," she repeated, bowing her head.

That would be a very great waste, he thought. After a moment, he found himself speaking. "Would you consider volunteering in the hospital?" He frowned. Where had that idea come from?

Her head had come up at his offer, her eyes wide and brilliant blue. "This is a Yankee hospital," she said in a voice that quivered with strong emotion. "I will not volunteer." She turned her gaze away for a moment, then looked again at him. "I must be paid a salary."

"Paid?" What a strange notion. Then he remembered that there still was an opening on the hospital staff. "Yes, of course you shall be paid. Ward Three needs a matron. Would that position be of interest?"

Her eyes lit. "What would that require?"

He searched his memory. "You would be in charge of two nurses and oversee the comfort of patients as they convalesce. Make sure they have proper bedding and sufficient food." He saw her interest waning. "Also, escort them to take the air. Write letters." Hope faded from her face. "Change bandages?" he ventured.

"I suppose it must suffice," she murmured.

Alex shrank from her disdain. How much better had been the light he had brought to her eyes earlier! How could he save the situation?

"We can start with those duties, so you may become accustomed to our 'Yankee' ways," he said, rashly considering taking her into the operating suite with him. Doctor Kellner would surely dismiss him from his position out of hand were he to do so.

"That will serve, to begin," she said, looking at him again.

Had animation returned to her being? "Very good. When will you be available?"

"Tomorrow," she said, her voice decisive.

"And your headaches?"

"I feel very well." She raised her chin.

Alex noted that now her eyes sparkled. Yes. *What will tomorrow bring?*

Alex stood and accompanied Mrs. Owen to his office door, then watched as she walked down the corridor and opened the door to the vestibule to depart. His body felt as though it buzzed. He hadn't felt this much physical attraction to a woman since the last day he had seen Cassie alive. He stopped his thoughts from going in that direction. Cassie was dead.

He recalled fuzzy images from the dream he'd had the night he arrived in Charlottesville. He'd thought the dream must have to do with Cassie, since he'd been feeling particularly guilty over coming here, abandoning his past, their past, as it were. But no. The woman in the dream had not resembled Cassie in coloration. Nor did she have a curvaceous form like Cassie's. The woman— His excitement heightened. The woman had been light complected, slim, with golden hair. Hair like that of Mrs. Owen. The Widow Owen.

The stubborn, very-much-bereaved Widow Owen.

His excitement abated. There was no point in

thinking of a future relationship of any romantic kind with Mrs. Owen. And yet, he'd had a dream, and he was now convinced that it had dealt with Mrs. Owen.

Perhaps the dream had not foretold a future together, but had only meant he would meet a woman to hire as a matron. He threw up his hands and remembered that he should inform Doctor Kellner that the position of matron had been filled. Grabbing his coat, he shrugged into it and made his way to the Director's office.

Ella Ruth felt the smile lifting the corners of her mouth as she pushed open the vestibule door, then the outside door, and looked for the buggy. Thomas waited patiently beside it, several yards away, and she walked toward him.

I have a position, a job of work to do. I am to receive a salary! No longer would she need to fret over her father's possible death. She would have money to put by, money to sustain her and her mother in the event of such a tragedy. She would be engaged in useful work each day. Then she remembered an added benefit, and her smile increased as Thomas handed her into the buggy. *I won't have to go visiting with Momma.*

Sitting in the parlor after dinner, Ella Ruth could find no pretext for bringing up the fact that she now had a position at the new hospital until Momma asked how her visit had gone.

Ella Ruth carefully composed her face and lifted her chin. "It went rather well, indeed. I met with a Doctor Marshall, and he arrived at a remedy for my headaches." She paused, knowing Momma would not be able to contain her curiosity.

"And what is that, Daughter?" Momma's face looked pinched.

"I am to do useful work."

"What sort of work?" Her father's interest had been piqued at last.

"Hospital work. I was given the position of matron on a ward."

"But you canno—"

"Do remember that I worked with Uncle Joseph in the Mount Jackson hospital, Poppa."

"But that was different!" Her father rose to his feet. Merlin sat placidly with his legs crossed at the knees, smoking his pipe and hiding behind a newspaper. Momma's face went pale, probably with apprehension, Ella Ruth thought.

She let the silence build, as her father began to pace. Finally she spoke. "How so?"

He drew to a halt in front of her. "It was war time. We each did what we could to advance the cause. You were assisting your uncle."

"I worked in a hospital, relieving suffering. It is no different."

"But it's a Yankee hospital!" her father sputtered.

Ella Ruth began to laugh. Poppa looked puzzled. Momma said, "Oh my." Merlin snorted from his side of the room.

She stifled her laughter in order to say, "You have made much to-do about my being sociable with the Yankees, Poppa. At the hospital, I shall be right in the midst of them." She paused to wipe her eyes with a muslin handkerchief. "Besides, I shall receive a salary for my work. I will put it away against need."

"I suppose we can let her do this for a trial period, Theo." Momma looked uncertain.

Her father made a scoffing noise, deep in his throat. "Her mind is made up, Louisa. You'll never be able to get her to stop."

Ella Ruth rose, triumph making her bosom expand. "Good night. I must be at the hospital early." She left the buzz of her parents' voices behind in the parlor and climbed the stairs to her room. She would never have to visit a Yankee household again.

Chapter 5

"What on earth have I gotten myself into?" Ella Ruth whispered to herself the next morning as she debated upon what a "Matron" would wear in a Yankee hospital. She began to pace the room, attired only in her shift. Nothing came to mind. The doctor had given her no instructions, no advisement at all except for an arrival time. If she didn't solve her attire dilemma soon, she would be late. She was already cold. Heaven forfend she should start to shiver before she even left the house.

Lula stood patiently at the open door of the wardrobe, silently awaiting her direction.

Ella Ruth turned and strode toward Lula, whose eyebrows had risen expectantly in the last few moments. The girl would soon give an exasperated huff and adopt a less restrained attitude. Ella Ruth threw up her hands.

"What do I wear?" she asked. "I have no experience of Yankee hospitals."

"Your uncle, Doctor Allen, he didn't complain none when you wore your ordinary dresses," Lula said, her expression starting to harden.

"All right. All right," Ella Ruth conceded. "Find me something."

When Lula touched the skirt of the dress Momma had brought into her room last week, a purple dress made of lawn and sprigged with white flowers, Ella Ruth burst out, "No!" and then took a breath and thought better of railing at her servant. "It's not warm enough," she said in a more moderate tone. That was true enough. Momma meant for her to wear it come spring.

Lula had the temerity to grin. "I's joking with you, Missy. Here's your old wool skirt, plenty good for the Yankees and with wear enough in it for the whole winter."

Ella Ruth nodded, not sure whether she should be outraged or thankful that Lula could dredge up a sense of humor for the occasion. The black skirt would suit. She could wear the black bodice from yesterday, as well.

"I reckon you'll want this apron, Missy," Lula said as she held up a very large white number that surely came out of Cook's wardrobe.

"Where did you get that?"

Lula chuckled. "Cook has three. She won't miss this one."

Ella Ruth felt her nerves settling. Of course she should wear a protective garment over her clothing. Who knew what she would encounter at the hospital? Soiled bandages always made a mess, and if any of the Yankees suffered from illness instead of wounds, there might be more unpleasantness to face.

"Thank you, Lula," she said, and her shoulders relaxed. She gave her head a tentative shake. No pain. Perhaps hard work was to be the cure for her headaches.

Ella Ruth opened the door to the hospital vestibule and stopped, listening to the buggy driving off under Thomas's hand, leaving her behind. For a moment, she regretted letting Thomas go. Perhaps it was unwise of her to come here in the first place.

After a moment, she remembered Dr. Marshall's seeming disbelief that she had assisted in Uncle Joseph's surgery in Mount Jackson. Yes, the young doctor had hidden it well, but she was sure he thought she had been overstating her experience. He would learn that she had not exaggerated. If not today, upon some future occasion.

Bolstered with pride in her past accomplishments, she walked through the vestibule, into the hall, and down the passageway toward Dr. Marshall's office.

She carried a woven basket that contained not only her lunch, but a small kit of bandages, salves, and liniment. Perhaps they would prove useful, perhaps not. That depended upon the stock of supplies the Yankees had on hand.

The door to the room stood open, held in that position by a brass doorstop of considerable size. It was made in the likeness of a dog, its head turned, alert. She supposed it was a retriever of some kind, and wondered if Dr. Marshall enjoyed the sport of hunting.

She could ask him, as he was sitting at his desk looking at a stack of papers, but it was not a matter that bore any weight upon her work. Besides, no one had been engaged in hunting for some years.

She brought up her chin as she realized she was wrong. Yankees had hunted down her countrymen as though they were vermin. Thus armed with a prickly attitude, she stepped into the room.

The doctor looked up, saw it was her, and smiled.

He bore a dimple in his right cheek.

His welcoming air took her by surprise. She had not expected to be welcome, seeing that she was a Southern woman of somewhat questionable veracity.

She answered his smile with a brief attempt at her own, which stretched her mouth in long-unused directions and felt like the rictus of death. Perhaps it was better to remain stolid rather than to appear foolish.

"Good morning." Dr. Marshall stood and beamed at her, motioning to the chair in front of his desk that she had cleared of papers the day before. "Please sit down. I will send for Doctor Kellner. He is our director, of the hospital, I mean."

She did so, murmuring a "good morning" of her own as she reached upward to raise her mourning veil before she remembered that she had not worn it today in anticipation of performing manual labor. She let her arms slide into her lap, wondering how odd she seemed to the doctor. She hoped she was not blushing.

The doctor stepped into the hall and hailed someone at a distance. "Do find French— That is, Doctor Kellner, and bring him here, won't you?" After a pause, his voice called out again. "And Nurse Gordon, too, if you can locate her."

He came back inside the room, sweeping his fingers through his black hair, front to back, in what seemed to be an attempt to tame a lock of it that had previously resided upon his brow.

Ella Ruth smiled to herself. She had seen other boys do the same. Men, she meant. She had seen other men do that same gesture. Although he was older than her by a number of years, Doctor Marshall was not the elderly physician she had expected to meet yesterday. All previous doctors and surgeons of her acquaintance were of advanced years, with an abundance of facial hair. This man could not be more than ten years her senior, if that. And his face was refreshingly clean-shaven.

The doctor resumed his place behind the desk and again smiled at her. The dimple made a reappearance.

Ella Ruth squirmed. *I should not be thinking of another man's appearance, and certainly not that of a Yankee!* But there was about him an air of confidence and good cheer that attracted her notice. He had not treated her poorly, as a victor might treat a conquered woman. Although he clearly didn't think of her as his equal, he had been more than pleasant to her.

The thought should have reassured her. Instead, her chest tightened. She was a widow, and she must remember that here. She must comport herself with the dignity befitting the reality that she was the relic of the late and very lamented Benjamin Owen, even if she disliked the sound of that word. Relic. It sounded like she was old and wizened.

". . . and that is the order of supervision in this hospital."

Ella Ruth compressed her lips. The doctor had been addressing her, and she had failed to listen.

"I will be your immediate supervisor, but you should meet the Director today so that you may recognize him." He smiled again and jumped to his feet at the sound of steps in the hallway.

A man suitably attired in a well-cut suit, with the

requisite gray whiskers and pinch spectacles perched atop his nose, bustled into the room.

"And here he is," Dr. Marshall announced, moving out from behind the desk to shake the man's hand.

I can see that for myself.

The newcomer peered at Ella Ruth over the top of his spectacles, then turned slightly toward Dr. Marshall. "This is the young lady?" he asked in a pronounced French accent.

Dr. Marshall nodded.

"And she claims experience?"

"Yes. She seems very competent."

Dr. Kellner turned to face Ella Ruth. "I am the Director. I am pleased to make the acquaintance," he said with an approximation of a bow.

"As am I," Ella Ruth murmured with an actual inclination of her head. The man almost chugged with energy, anxious to be on his way again.

"I will leave you in Doctor Marshall's hands," he replied, and exited, muttering something about "rounds".

Ella Ruth look toward Dr. Marshall, who paused as though he were waiting for something, then laughed. "And he is gone," he said when he had finished. "Doctor Kellner is never still for long."

"He does seem most energetic," she answered.

"He is a capable surgeon, trained in Europe. He's Belgian by birth, not French, as we all had supposed when we met him."

"And you call him 'Frenchy' behind his back?"

Dr. Marshall appeared thunderstruck. "You heard

me? I suppose I did slip when I sent the orderly to fetch him." He wagged his finger in front of Ella Ruth's nose. "Never to his face, mind you. Never to his face." He pulled a pocket watch from his vest pocket and frowned at it. "Where is that confounded woman?"

"I beg your pardon?"

"Excuse me. I lack manners. I'm not referring— I expected— The nurse should be here by now."

"The nurse?"

"Nurse Gordon. I mentioned her before, you know. She will show you the supplies and explain our procedures."

"Oh. Yes." I should have been listening.

"And here she is." Dr. Marshall repeated a version of his unnecessary announcement as a tall, robust woman entered the office.

Ella Ruth stood to be introduced to the woman, whose auburn tresses were arranged in coils beneath a sort of mob cap. She was taller than Ella Ruth, but not as tall as Dr. Marshall, who smiled, again displaying his dimple.

"Mrs. Owen, may I present Miss Miriam Gordon? Nurse Gordon, this is Mrs. Benjamin Owen, who is to be our matron for Ward Three. Please take her around the hospital, show her the storage room and the linen room, and see that she knows her responsibilities."

"Thank you, Doctor," the woman replied, then looked at Ella Ruth. "Will you be leaving after I show you around, ma'am?"

"No. No, I mean to begin, today."

The woman smiled. "That is good. We worried that

the position would remain open for some time for a lack of reliable applicants. Your appearance is like a miracle, ma'am."

Ella Ruth tilted her head slightly. "I'm not a miracle, Nurse Gordon, but I am industrious and, I hope, enterprising."

"That is good, ma'am." She turned to Dr. Marshall and nodded her head. "We'll be on our way now, Doctor. I'll take good care of Mrs. Owen." She led the way to the door, and Ella Ruth followed in her wake, turning her head before she passed through the open doorway.

"Thank you, Doctor."

His eyes lit up and he smiled. "My pleasure, Miss—uh, Mrs. Owen."

Alex stood in his office, feeling again the clutch of excitement he'd nearly forgotten existed. He'd told Mrs. Owen it had been a pleasure to— what? To serve her? Of course. That was his job.

To see her?

Yes. He had taken pleasure in that. From the moment he had met her, it had been a pleasure to deal with her and to see her: face, form, figure and all. His only disappointment was in her rigid formality in regards to him. She seemed resolute in her decision to put herself apart from humanity, or at least from the thought of cultivating a relationship with a man other than her deceased husband.

In all truthfulness, he understood the range of her emotions upon losing a loved one. Hadn't he fallen apart inside when he received Mother's letter about Cassie's death? Hadn't he soothed his pain in temporary bouts with the liquor bottle, until the grief subsided after long months? He still felt a twinge of sorrow upon occasion, and would always carry the guilt of not saving her life, which he knew was thoroughly irrational.

But he didn't understand Mrs. Owen's desire to withdraw entirely from life in polite society. Yes, it had not been a year yet since her man had fallen, but should the boundaries of one's grief be counted in days, weeks, months, years? He had come through the bad time in less than a year. Might not Mrs. Owen, as well?

He didn't want to examine the frisson of pleasure being in the woman's presence had brought. She was not willing to do more than her duties. She only wanted to earn a salary—for what purpose, he did not know. Until she was ready to lose her hold on widowhood, he could not entice her to experience the same excitement, and yes, attraction, as he did.

He shook his head and went back to his stack of medical reports and notes on the patients' progress. Mrs. Owen was a puzzle, but he was going to enjoy having her around the hospital.

By the end of the day, Ella Ruth's head whirled with instructions. How was she ever to remember so many details, so many patients? The faces of the men who were recovering from battle wounds haunted her. If Ben had lived, would he have carried such visible signs of anguish?

Nurse Gordon left her at the bedside of a man who clearly was not going to live much longer. Before she went home, Ella Ruth was to write a letter for him, putting down his words of love to his wife. It proved to be a difficult, emotional task.

She wasn't sure she could have borne to read a final letter from Ben like the one Mr. Christopher William Bryant dictated to her. She had received a note from Ben written before the battle at Waynesboro. There was no intimation that it was to be his last. She waited in vain for another. At least Mrs. Bryant would have the comfort of one last message from her beloved.

The soldier took a likeness of his wife from under his pillow and shared it with Ella Ruth. At one time in her life, she would have called the woman homely. Instead, she recognized the resolute steadfastness in her face. Mr. Bryant spoke so lovingly of the woman that she barely held back her tears. She agreed with him that she was indeed a remarkable woman, and envied her the love that her husband bore her, and that he was yet alive to express it through Ella Ruth's hand.

When the letter was finished and Mr. Bryant—she did not know his rank—fell into a restless slumber, Ella Ruth didn't know what to do with the missive to his wife. Nurse Gordon was not around, so she finally decided to take it to Dr. Marshall's office. If he was there, he could give her instructions on how to post it.

He seemed to be a generous man, at least he had been so to her up to now. He always had greeted her with a smile and a noted lack of condescension toward her in her position of conquered Southern woman. Was it possible for some Yankees to be good men? Perhaps. She would reserve judgement until she had a better knowledge of him.

A rap came on his office door, and Alex shouted "Come in."

The door opened. Mrs. Owen appeared, followed his directive, and approached the desk, holding a folded piece of paper.

He leaped to his feet, a grin tugging at his cheeks. "Come in!"

"I am in," she replied, ducking her head so that he barely caught sight of a tiny smile.

She had left her widow's veil at home, thankfully, and must have removed her bonnet in order to move about the ward more freely. Such lovely hair, burnished gold. He wished it were down. He would have liked to see its full glory.

"Yes. I see." It was grand to see her more comfortable. "Did Nurse Gordon acquaint you with the workings of the ward?"

"She did, spending several hours showing me around before she left me at the side of a patient. I wrote out a letter for the man, a soldier who, I fear, is not doing well. How shall I post it?" Her voice became hushed. "It is directed to his wife. It may be his last."

"That's unfortunate," he said, and put out his hand. "I will take charge of it. You needn't worry about sending it."

"I should like to know how it is done. Surely it won't

be the only letter I'll write for one of the patients. Dying or otherwise."

"Yes. I see that would be important knowledge for you to have." He invited her to seat herself and then acquainted her with the process. When he had finished, he asked, "Do you anticipate any difficulties with the work?"

"I am competent to manage it."

He had no doubt of it. He imagined she wanted more challenging tasks, such as going into surgery. *That won't happen soon, my girl,* he thought, then raised his eyebrows at his temerity in using that term in regards to their relationship.

"You seem in doubt, Doctor."

"I beg your pardon?"

"Doubt is often expressed with raised eyebrows."

He lifted a stack of papers on his desk to another spot before he answered. "As is surprise, Mrs. Owen, but my surprise was not directed at you. I had an errant thought." *Which I had better keep well hidden.* "I am gratified that you are so readily grasping hold of what we do here."

"I was given simple duties."

"I cannot offer you more at this time." How he wished he could. He would like to see what she could do with the knife under his direction. He imagined what it would be like to escort such a comely woman to an officer's ball. Now that would be a sight. She would outshine any other woman there!

"Your mind is preoccupied with other matters, Doctor. Thank you for informing me of the procedure for the mail." She paused a moment before rising from her seat to leave. "No doubt I shall see you tomorrow."

"I look forward to the pleasure," he said, meaning it.

Chapter 6

Ella Ruth thrived on mastering the duties of ward matron, and soon felt at home assigning Nurse Gordon and the second nurse in her charge, Nurse Gilly, specific tasks, which she modified to suit her sense of appropriateness. There was no complaint from the other two ward matrons once she explained her reasons for wanting to change procedures, such as bundling the linens together. She pointed out that if there were an emergency need to change a bed, picking up a bundle of two sheets and a pillowcase was more efficient than taking the time to pull separate items from different stacks in the linen room.

In exchange, Ella Ruth found herself learning much from Nurse Gordon, who had served as a nurse during most of the war years. As they worked closely together caring for their patients, the woman asked her to call her 'Miriam' in private conversations, and Ella Ruth agreed to do it. She hadn't yet overcome the sense of propriety that had her insisting that she be addressed as Matron, though.

"Matron," Nurse Gordon asked one day. "Have you thought to pray with the unfortunate souls who will soon be passing on?"

"Pray?" Ella Ruth felt a twinge of unease. Her family did not hold private devotions at home, and she was unaccustomed to the practice.

"Perhaps we cannot save all the patients, ma'am, but we can send them off to the Good Lord's care and keeping with a prayer of comfort in their ears."

The conversation led to much thinking on Ella Ruth's part. Had her spiritual education been insufficient? She knew Ben's family was devout, but she thought prayers were the proper province of the ministers. She began to experiment at night with a sort of intimate discourse with God.

A month later, Ella Ruth's efficiencies reached the ears of Dr. Kellner, who complimented her on her good sense. "I like enterprise. I like saving time. There is not enough of it in a day, *non*?" He touched her arm in a familiar manner.

She had to bite her tongue to keep from blurting out, "Then two more hands in the surgery would be a time saver, yes?" But she had no idea whether or not Dr. Marshall had mentioned that portion of her experience to the director. In all likelihood, he had not, despite his seeming to hold her in high regard in other matters.

He, too, had complimented her, but on an entirely different sort of area.

"Your color has improved," he said out of the blue one day in March.

She had stared at him, slightly discomfited. Such a remark had no place in their doctor-matron relationship. "Why do you mention that?"

"You are my patient for the headaches," he said.

"Oh. Perhaps you should discharge me. They are no longer a bother."

His face had beamed at her words. "Very good. I am

delighted to hear it."

More worrisome, today he came into the ward, still wearing a bloody apron from the operatory, took her aside, and asked if he might come to her home and have an interview with her parents.

His request surprised her, but more than that, she feared his motivation. "Why would you do that?" she asked.

"I would like to inform them of your good progress as a matron at the hospital, and, of course, to give them the important news that your health has improved." He grinned.

She tried not to look at the dimple in his cheek while she searched her brain for a reason to put him off. *I don't want him to know the location of my residence.* At length, she could find no fault in his explanation and no excuse for why he should not meet her parents, and reluctantly gave him directions.

"Would Friday evening suit your father?"

"Umm," she vocalized, wondering if Northern doctors did not send a calling card ahead, requesting an interview. Probably not. Northern manners had other boundaries. "Six o'clock is a good time to catch Poppa at home before supper."

"Has he a name?"

She blinked. "A name?" Oh. She had called him only "Poppa." "Yes, of course. He is Theodore Allen. My mother is Louisa. I have a brother named Merlin." She wondered why she was babbling on.

"And you are?" His eyes twinkled.

"Mrs. Benjamin Owen."

"Have you your own name? I've never heard it, and you've been working here for some months."

She raised her chin. Why should he want to know her Christian name?

A slow smile crept over his face. "I am Alexander, but I use the shorter name Alex with my associates."

Does he count me among his associates? She wished he wouldn't smile.

"What may I call you when 'Mrs. Owen' or 'Matron' do not suit?"

When would there be a time that her husband's name or the word "matron" would not suit? Her heart rebelled against revealing her own name, but he still smiled at her.

"I—" She stopped and looked at the toes of her shoes, then breathed in the mixed odors of blood from his apron and bay rum from his person. Her father smelled of the latter after visiting his barber. Her father wanted her to be friendly to the Yankees of her acquaintance. She swallowed down her annoyance, raised her head and said, "I am called Ella Ruth."

"Ella Ruth Owen." His smile became a ghost.

"Yes."

"I will see you at home on Friday." He turned away, the clipped words echoing in her ears, and she wondered what had soured his mood.

Alex walked away, exited the ward and fled to his office.

Ella Ruth. She will always be Ella Ruth Owen,

Benjamin Owen's widow. I have no chance.

He yanked open the door, closed it just as brusquely, and threw himself into his chair. He swiveled it from the office so he could gaze out the window. Dr. Kellner's carriage rolled toward the street. The realization that he would have to cover the director's afternoon operation rankled, which increased his melancholia.

A rap came at the door. Alex swiveled the chair toward his desk. "Come in," he said, rather more loudly than needed.

Mrs. Costain, the matron from Ward Two, entered and stood before the desk, waiting.

He wished she was the matron of Ward Three instead, but she was not. Hunching himself downward in his chair, he growled, "What do you need?"

At her wide-eyed reaction, he amended, "Matron," in a more seemly tone, and sat taller. "How may I help you?"

"I need your signature for the burial of Private Wells," she said, laying a bundle of paper on his desk. "I cannot locate the Director."

"He is out," he replied, trying not to let his annoyance show in his voice. He found a pencil among the mounds of paper on the desk, scribbled his signature, and shoved the papers back to the Matron. "Please prepare a letter of condolence to the private's parents. If the Director is not in the hospital when you are finished, bring it here and I'll sign it."

"I have done that," the woman answered, shuffled the top paper aside, and presented the letter to him.

"Matron Owen said it is more convenient to take all the necessary papers to the Director at one time. Or to you, in this case, Doctor."

Alex read the letter. It was written in a different hand than the order for burial, and he wondered if Ella— Mrs. Owen had written it. He nodded approval of the contents, then pulled a drawer open, took from it a nib pen and an ink well, and signed the letter with the more formal ink.

"Thank you, Matron. Mrs. ah, Owen has creative thoughts on how to make the work easier. You are wise to heed them."

"Yes, even though she's a rebel through and through," the woman answered, a touch of harshness in her tone.

"The war is over, Matron."

"I don't think it is, for her," she answered, and picked up the papers. "She doesn't let it go." She left the room, hugging the papers to her chest.

"I wonder when she will, if ever?" he muttered, letting his shoulders slump once more. "Ella Ruth." He said her name on a sigh, then sat bolt upright. It was time to quit pretending and acknowledge that his physical attraction to the woman had ripened into a caring that surpassed the feeling he had held for his dead fiancée. Cassie was gone, and he had been fond of her. He had mourned her loss, blamed himself for not being at home to cure her. But he had not *loved* her.

He swallowed. The warmth he felt for Ella Ruth Owen was more than physical desire. It was a yearning to keep her safe always, to protect her, to hold her close forever. He loved her. He must find a way to express his devotion, a way in which she could acknowledge his worth at the same time as she honored her dead husband.

"We are the sum of our experiences," he muttered. "The griefs we have borne must not lessen us. They must point us to caring hearts that carry us forward."

He wondered if some philosopher had first expressed those thoughts, or if they were unique to him.

He put his hands on the desktop, levered himself upright, and went to see about Dr. Kellner's afternoon appointments.

All the rest of the week, Ella Ruth found herself thinking of Dr. Marshall's impending visit with her parents. Was the state of her employment and her health his real motivation for seeking the appointment? More than one time since she had begun her employment, she had caught him observing her closely, with what seemed to be a frank personal interest. One or two times, she caught him standing in the doorway leading to the corridor when he had no reason to be in the ward. He would glance her way, his eyes filled with admiration, then quickly leave, the double doors swinging in his wake.

Ben had cast such admiring glances her way. Having Dr. Marshall do so made her intensely uneasy. She had made sure that the nurses under her charge knew of her desire to remain a widow, so there would be no idle talk. His attention to her as a woman threatened her intention to remain employed at the hospital as a hedge against her father's death, and, if possible, to gain the doctor's trust so that she could once again assist in doing surgeries.

Having no alternative scheme for earning wages, she increased in anxiety until on Thursday, she had to send Thomas to the hospital with a message that she was bedridden with headache.

At mid-morning, Lula shook her awake. "Missy, wake up. Your doctor man is here. He say he's going to examine you."

Ella Ruth tried to open her eyes, attempting to fight back a rising panic. "No. Tell him no, Lula. He must not come here."

"Your mama say she will show him up to your room. You better get dressed."

Dizzy with the pain that had not receded during her sleep, she shook her head with careful motion. "He cannot enter my bedroom, Lula."

"I can't keep him away, Missy. Your mama is firm set that he is coming up to cure the headache." She shook her head. "Why you got a headache now? It be months since you last had one."

"The doctor planned to call on Poppa and Momma tomorrow night." She tried to ease her limbs out from under the covers. "I fear his motives."

"Is he a good-lookin' man, this doctor of yours?"

"Oh Lula, don't talk nonsense," she rallied. "He's not *my* doctor. He's merely my supervisor at the hospital." She turned her head. Was that a heavy footstep on the stair? "Is he coming?"

"I reckon that be him. You better get back in bed and cover yourself."

Thinking Lula gave wise counsel, Ella Ruth managed to get herself back under the bedding and in a prone position before Dr. Marshall charged through the door, her mother close behind.

"What is this?" Alex demanded, his voice sounding brusque in his ears. "Why are you abed?"

Ella Ruth looked up at him. Her eyes appeared to be out of focus. He didn't let her answer.

"Have you taken a fall? Are you concussed?"

Fear for her health muddled his mind and sharpened his tone. She had told him she no longer was plagued with the headaches. Why had this one come upon her? *Have I done something—?*

"I—" She blinked and her eyes seemed to focus. She looked at Mrs. Allen. "You have met my mother."

"Indeed I have. She graciously allowed me to see you." He turned toward the mother. "Thank you, ma'am. I will tend most carefully to your daughter." The woman eyed him appraisingly, then nodded and left the room.

He turned again toward Ella Ruth, noting that the maid had not moved from her post on the other side of the bed. "Your mother insisted, in fact, that I see you. What has caused this attack? Have you felt it coming on?"

"I don't— That is to say, I have been concerned about your visit tomorrow. The anxiety must have caused me sufficient stress to—" Her voice ceased.

"Why on earth would you be concerned?"

She turned her face away from him, and he knew she was embarrassed by his coming.

In a low tone he said, "I would not for the world give you stress, Miss— Mrs. Owen. As your doctor, I was concerned when I heard you are ill."

"Why?" She looked directly at him again.

The question took him aback. Did she question his concern as a doctor? Her doctor? Wasn't it natural for him to be worried over the return of the attacks?

Has she guessed that my concern for her welfare is personal?

He looked down at her, lying so still in the bed. He was helpless to declare his true feelings, stifled by his role as her superior and by her adamant refusal to see him as a man, besides. How long would this stalemate endure? How could he persuade her to leave off her sorrow and come back to life?

He bent over the bed. "He must have been a remarkable man," he murmured so low that only Mrs. Owen would hear him.

Her eyes opened wide. Then they misted over.

"No other man can rise to his level," she answered, her voice equally low.

He longed to say, "I would like to make the attempt," but feared she would shrink from him and all trust between them would be lost.

Alex stood erect. "Continue with cold compresses and sleep, and use this powder, as well," he said in a doctorly tone, and placed a number of patent medicine packets on the table beside her bed. "I will instruct your maid in their use," he said, and turned to leave the room. The sound of footsteps told him the maid was following.

He thought he heard Mrs. Owen reply, but he was too far away to hear her clearly. He continued out the door, wondering what she had said.

He wants to supplant Ben in my heart.

The insight filled Ella Ruth's body with pain, even as she battled the ache in her head.

He has formed an attraction for me. His anxious demeanor had told her that, as clearly as if he had said so aloud. When he had interviewed her in the first instance about her headaches, he had been grave in his concern, as befitted him as a doctor. Today he had all but fallen on his knees to pledge his undying affection for her.

She knew the power of attraction, of affection, of love. Didn't her love for Ben keep her safe from all incursions into her private thoughts and memories? Spare her the pain of any other loss?

All she wanted was to perform her duties at the hospital, receive her just payment, and otherwise close out the world so she could remember Ben. She recalled his touch upon her body, the pleasures they had shared, the private ecstasies known to no others but them. She had experienced passion in abundance. Ben had given her that gift. But Ben was gone. She had to close that part of herself away in a sanctuary of memories, wrap her passion away within a cocoon of iron. She must guard that no other man could open that door, not even a well-put-together doctor with a dimpled cheek.

She turned on her side, facing away from the door in case he should return.

How was she to return to the hospital, knowing that he bore her affection? She needed her wages. She needed to be useful to the men on her ward, broken men trying to become whole. She needed respect and approval. She didn't need affection from Doctor Marshall.

She heard a step on the stair and peered over her shoulder, breathing more rapidly than normal. No one opened her door. She tried to regulate the unseemly quickness of her heartbeat, but it took a while to settle into a normal rate.

Poor Doctor Marshall! She almost pitied him. She could not let him close, could not let him make an assault on her citadel of impassioned memories. She would not betray her love for Ben, even for a good man, as she now knew him to be. He would have to find another, a less broken woman with whom to build a life.

Am I broken? She hadn't thought of herself as being broken for a while now, not since she had regained a sense of worth due to her work. Alex Marshall had taken a chance and offered her a position at the hospital after she refused to volunteer. Alex had smiled and approved her changes in the management of the ward. Even Dr. Kellner had been happy with her innovations. But Alex had given her the start.

Alex?

"No," she moaned. "I am always and forever Ben's woman."

Chapter 7

Ella Ruth returned to the hospital when her headache ceased, hesitantly at first, then with more assurance as Dr. Marshall kept out of her way. *He has seen the futility of seeking a more abiding friendship,* she thought. *That suits me.*

The work with the stricken men gratified her, especially as she saw the health of individuals improve under her care. Not all of them had battle wounds to contend with. Many of them suffered from various illnesses that had lingered past the close of fighting. A few had consumption and other ills. But many had festering wounds that needed constant care.

One such was a Private O'Meara, who had been sent to the hospital for treatment of a lung ailment. During his long stay, he had neglected to mention an infection in his big toe that developed from an ingrown toenail. By the time Ella Ruth discovered the man in great pain, gangrene had taken over his toe, and sepsis was threatening his life. She mentioned the situation to Dr. Kellner, who said he would keep an eye on the case.

A day later, the boy was almost comatose. Livid, Ella Ruth sent Nurse Gordon to bring Dr. Marshall, but he was doing a delicate surgery. Dr. Kellner was not in the hospital that day.

"The toe must come off immediately," she told the nurse when she returned. "It's poisoning the poor boy."

"I told you the doctors are not available."

Ella Ruth tapped her foot in frustration. "It must be removed today." She looked at Miriam. "Are you willing to help this brave soldier survive?"

"Of course."

"Then you must lend me a hand. I can remove the toe. It's not a complex procedure. I have assisted with such work many times."

"You, ma'am?"

"I was my uncle's assistant." She saw doubt in Miriam's pursed lips. "My uncle is a surgeon of top rank. He took me into the surgery of the hospital in Mount Jackson to assist him. I can do this and save the man's life."

"Doctor Kellner will discharge us both for overstepping our bounds."

"He may do so, but we will first save Private O'Meara's life. That fact will speak for itself in our defense."

Getting a reluctant agreement from Nurse Gordon, Ella Ruth prepared the patient, took him into the second operatory, sedated him, and removed the toe, which she preserved in a glass jar.

"Have you a procedure for the disposal of medical wastes?"

Alex rose from his chair and nodded to Ella Ruth, who had rushed into his office, carrying a glass jar. "Slops, you mean."

"No. I deal with slops every day." She held up the

jar, which contained a black object in a few inches of liquid. "I mean tissue. Do you burn it or bury it?"

"Where did you get that? There have been no surgeries scheduled in the past week." His temper flared briefly, then he endeavored without success to suppress it. What had the woman done?

She raised her chin slightly. "I borrowed a bone saw a week ago and took this gangrenous toe off Private O'Meara's foot. He is much improved now."

"Miss Allen!" Immediately he knew he'd blurted out the name he wished she bore.

"Mrs. Owen." She narrowed her brows and glared at him.

He glared back, then thumped his fist on the desk. "You are not authorized to perform surgery. Take me to the man."

Ella Ruth stood her ground. "Not until you answer my question."

"I'll have Hobbs give it a decent burial." Alex leaned forward across the desk and reached for the jar, which she kept from him.

"Then you bury waste?"

"Yes." He snorted. "We have a lovely patch at the back of the hospital garden." He moved around the desk and held out his hand.

This time Ella Ruth allowed him to take the toe jar, which he set on the desk. "I think you'll find Private O'Meara's temperature has fallen significantly. He is now on the way to regaining his health."

"And you believe you brought that about?"

"Of course I did. If Doctor Kellner will not act to

save a life, as I suggested he do, and you are not available in the moment of need, I must do whatever is in my power to protect my patients." She brushed her hands together to signify completion of a task.

Alex's mood changed as he saw the satisfaction evident in her motion, and he chuckled. *What an admirable woman she is.* "The Director will not take kindly to your action in this situation. He could make a complaint." But who would he complain to? The health authorities in Washington City? They were far away and wouldn't care.

He looked at the blackened flesh in the specimen jar. "You do realize, Mrs. Owen, that you have preserved the life of a Yankee."

She stared at him for a long moment, then turned on her heel and said, "Come along if you wish to examine the patient."

He accompanied her to the ward, where he found Private O'Meara sitting up and playing cards with the man in the next bed.

"Well, Pat, let's take a look at that foot of yours," he said, and began to unwrap the bandages.

"Matron did a right good job keeping me from joining the haunts, Doctor."

He only grunted in reply as the foot came into view.

As he examined Ella Ruth's work, Alex marveled at the neatness of the job. The foot was pink and healthy, and new tissue had formed in the area of the sutures. They could come out in a few days. The woman was as experienced as she claimed. Having her in the operating suite would be a great advantage to his work. But he had never told Dr. Kellner of her supposed skills, and he doubted that the stubborn little director would value them as he did.

He led the way out of the ward and into the hall. "You did a pretty job," he said.

"I did. I am not ignorant of surgical procedures."

"You are not. Are you seeking my job?" he asked, half in jest.

"I would need more training to do it."

He raised an eyebrow. "I wish I could have you alongside me at the table. That's not in my power to grant."

"Is Doctor Kellner such an ogre?"

"He is set in his ways. He sees no potential in women as surgeons, I can assure you."

"But he is pleased with my work in the ward."

"You are a woman, and the work you do is woman's work. He's satisfied with that, but in his eyes, you are inferior to a man."

"Do you hold the same view?"

The challenge in her eyes shook him, and he didn't reply right away. He had to choose his words carefully. At last he found them.

"You have proven your worth. I hold your workmanship in high regard." *As I do your person.*

"Am I inferior to a man?"

"Decidedly not!" He felt some heat at the notion of Ella Ruth Owen being inferior in any way, and put it into his answer.

"Then find a way to put my skills to use and to train me further." She turned away and went into the ward.

Alex whistled in a low tone. That was another challenge. How he was to overcome it, he did not know.

Dr. Kellner continued to leave the hospital in the early afternoon, casting his work upon Alex. After a few weeks, Alex chafed at doing his own job and that of the Director as well. One day he confronted the man as he was trying to make his exit from a side door.

"Doctor, may I inquire why you're leaving? You're scheduled to remove Sergeant Belner's finger this afternoon."

The Director's widened eyes spoke of his surprise at being accosted. "I have an appointment. You will do the surgery."

"I can't. I have another surgery and much else to do today."

"You can postpone one or another operation." Dr. Kellner side-stepped to get around Alex, who did the same and blocked his path.

"Both patients are in a critical state. They can't be neglected. Look what happened with Private O'Meara."

"You did a fine job on him."

Alex paused before he answered. He had let Dr. Kellner assume that he had done the surgery himself, hoping to spare Mrs. Owen punishment or the loss of her employment.

"We need another surgeon if you're going to be absent so frequently."

"Then get someone in here. One of the town's surgeons, anyone! I cannot be here constantly."

That's your job. "I may ask whomever I please?"

"Whomever you please. Now let me proceed. I am late."

Alex stepped back, and then watched the man depart and hurry off on foot down the long driveway. *Whomever I please?* His heart lifted and he smiled at the Director's fleeing back. Mrs. Owen certainly was skilled enough to perform the removal surgery in Dr. Kellner's stead, and he had permission to ask anyone to do it. Anyone. Surely that included a beautiful woman with an excellent head on her shoulders and skilled hands.

An orderly came into the ward and informed Ella Ruth that she was wanted in Dr. Marshall's office. She passed off the bandage change she was doing to Nurse Gilly, washed the pus and blood off her hands, and went down the corridor.

She found Dr. Marshall pacing between his desk and the open door, and when she had seated herself at his bidding, he turned to her with a conspiratorial smile on his lips. He seemed ready to burst from excitement. "You're to remove Sergeant Belner's finger!"

She looked him up and down. "Doing so will place me in a precarious position, Doctor."

He cut her off. "I have the Director's permission. You can do the surgery. It's much like Private O'Meara's toe surgery, and you did that with dispatch."

"It was not complicated. Are you sure I may do this?"

"Dr. Kellner agreed that I might ask anyone. He insisted on it."

She narrowed her eyes. "Did you mention my name?"

He looked away. "Not precisely, but he was in a rush." He looked at her, but shifted his eyes away again. "The case is critical."

"And when he discovers a mere woman took on the surgery, will I be put out of my position?"

"I hope not," he muttered. "Come along, Mrs. Owen. Your patient is waiting."

Chapter 8

Several weeks later, a scandal descended on the hospital when Dr. Kellner resigned from his position and Dr. Marshall had to take over his duties.

From the whispers that swirled throughout the halls of the institution, Alex learned that the abrupt departure of Doctor Kellner stemmed from his wife's demand that they remove themselves from Charlottesville immediately. In just a few days, they left for the north, leaving much of their furniture and household items behind.

Alex speculated that the man's misfortune arose from misbehavior in his marriage, which might account for his unexplained absences during the daytime. It was a pity. Dr. Kellner was quite a brilliant surgeon, but mischief had sunk many a man's career before this.

On the other hand, the event might give him a boost in life. Should he be advanced into the director's position there would be an increase in salary. The director's position brought the power to staff the hospital as he deemed suitable for the best interests of the patients. But with the new position would come the need to play politics.

He hated politics, but every enterprise connected to the government was steeped in it, even the practice of medicine.

After a week, he got word that he was being

considered for the directorship. The supervisors in Washington City deemed him capable. Only the endless paperwork stood in the way of his advancement. If and when the appointment came through, they would require him to hire someone to fill his place. He was not inclined to wait. He wondered if such a contract as he had signed for Dr. Kellner would be binding upon Washington City.

He sat at his desk in the warm sunlight streaming through the office window, thinking over his possibilities.

Mrs. Owen had performed her assigned surgery in an exemplary manner. The sergeant recovered in good time, his health restored. *Do I dare offer her a position on the staff?* She was not qualified by study to serve as a surgeon, but he had no quarrel with her experience. Still, such a move as hiring an unqualified woman as surgeon would certainly raise a hubbub in the north. *Can I risk it?*

A perverse thought interrupted his musings. Might his chances to woo Mrs. Owen be improved should he give her charge over the second operating theatre? He sighed. Not necessarily. Mrs. Owen persisted in devotion to her martyred husband and would not be swayed into viewing Alex with romantic interest just because he rewarded her skills.

He had another choice. He knew of a young physician and surgeon in Charlottesville who was competent to serve on the hospital staff. Having another surgeon in the hospital would free Alex to give Mrs. Owen additional training.

She would work beside me. He felt his blood rise. Would she be a distraction to him instead of an advantage to the hospital? Was he serving only himself by keeping her close?

Perhaps it was so, but she wanted training. She deserved to have it. Who better than him to mold her into a real surgeon? Even if she never saw him as a man, she would have additional skills and the ability to make her way in an uncertain world. *I can give her that gift*, he decided.

Ella Ruth sat in stunned silence in Dr. Marshall's office as he offered to take her into his operatory as his assistant, to be trained as a surgeon.

Then he began to walk the well-beaten path between his desk and the door, waiting for her acceptance.

Are there conditions? What must I do in return?

Through lowered eyelashes, she watched him pace. Did he expect her to grant him some sort of liberties? Might the position come with a price she did not wish to pay?

"I cannot know if my father will pay for my training," she said. "He pays my brother's university fees already."

Dr. Marshall paced in silence.

"I am only his daughter, after all."

The doctor rounded on her, fierce emotion bristling his eyebrows. "Do you think I require payment to train you? The hospital will pay you as my assistant." He went back to pacing, muttering, "He should value you more."

"I am to be paid?"

"Of course," he growled from across the room.

"Why are you displeased with me?"

He stopped before her. "What do you mean?"

"You are angry. What can I think except that someone has forced you to make this offer? That you hate the notion."

His face softened. "I do not hate the notion. It's *my* notion, after all."

"It's your scheme?"

"You crave more knowledge. You deserve to have it."

"But I am a woman."

"Yes."

She rose to stand in front of him. "Why are you doing this?"

He looked uneasy and said nothing.

"Is it for your gain?"

"It benefits the hospital."

"But not you?"

"I direct the hospital at present."

She waited until he looked at her again. "But there is no gain for you?"

"Ella Ruth," he blurted out, "I want to give you your heart's desire. Training."

She stared at him. He had used her Christian name. "What are the strings attached? My person?"

He looked aghast.

"Do you have designs upon me?"

Dr. Marshall seemed rooted where he stood, his mouth half open, his face awash with emotion. After a long moment, he woodenly walked to the front of his desk and sat on the edge as though he could no longer stand. He spoke at last. "I bear you great affection. I believe you have discovered that. But I am not a man to take liberties, as you call such actions." He got off the desk and turned toward the window overlooking the front drive. "You do not wish to give your heart to another man. I don't understand that, but I will respect it. However, it pleases me to give you a gift, to share my knowledge."

Ella Ruth was shaken by his admission. For months she had suspected he had a personal interest in her, but he had never said anything. Now he owned up to his feelings, but instead of pressing her to consider him as a suitor, he freely offered her training in the medical arts, training as a surgeon. Could he really be that selfless?

She sought her chair and sat. She looked at her hands. She raised one and stroked the lump bulging beneath her bodice: her piece of broomstick, the proof of her marriage. She looked up to see Dr. Marshall gazing at her. He expected an answer. She looked down and stroked the finger of her hand that had never borne a ring from Ben, who had not been granted time to get her one. She stilled her hands in her lap and waited for inspiration as to how to make her answer. She swallowed.

"I accept your offer," she said, and burst into tears.

Alex knelt beside Ella Ruth's chair, watching her sob with her face in her hands, yearning to hold her, to comfort her, but knew he could not. He could take no such liberties, even to soothe whatever emotion had upset her. Had he not, scant moments before, as much as declared her to be off limits to him?

He remained beside her, his arms dangling like useless lengths of stove wood, wondering what caused her tears. She had withstood innumerable sorrows in her work, watching men wither and die, but she should be rejoicing at the advancement in her fortunes.

Should he try to pull her out of this sodden episode with a joke, a word of encouragement, an expression of his confidence in her? Perhaps it was best if he just knelt here to show his support of her, whatever the cause of her anguish.

And so he stayed in the same position, his knees going numb, until she fumbled in her pocket for a handkerchief and dabbed at her eyes with it.

"You're still here?" she questioned when at last she opened her eyes and saw him. "Don't you have duties?"

"Not at this moment," he mumbled.

She got to her feet, trembling. "I beg your pardon."

"For what?" He managed to get to his feet without making a fool of himself.

"For taking your time. For being a ninny."

"Well now—" He cleared his throat. "Nothing of the kind, Mrs. Owen." He wanted to wipe away a lingering teardrop hanging from her eyelash, but restrained himself, clasping his hands behind his back instead. He felt himself rising onto his toes, and immediately squelched the nervous response. Once he was firmly flat-footed again, he said, "You shall be 'Matron of the Operatory'."

She sniffed, whether from her bout with tears or in disdain, he did not know.

"I'm not to be named 'Assistant'?"

He waited a moment to admit his cowardice. "I dare not take long strides. The politicians have not confirmed me in my new place yet."

She turned her head aside. "How irksome it must be," she said, her tone flat.

"I dislike politics." I'd rather be a country physician, living down a country lane, with a comely woman as wife and assistant. He almost said it aloud, but shrank from alarming her.

"But you must play them?" She shook her head. "Of course you must." She sighed. "My father is obliged to play such games to get on, as well."

"There's dignity in surviving well," he said, and didn't know whether he meant Ella Ruth, her father, or himself.

"I believe my mother would say the same." She raised her chin and turned her gaze upon him. "When do I start?"

His inhalation expanded his chest to the extent that he felt revived again. He let it half-way out and said, "Tomorrow, as I have a surgery in the morning. I'll give Nurse Gordon your position."

"She has earned it," she said, and left his office.

Chapter 9

Ella Ruth began her duties feeling as though she hung on a silken strand somewhere between heaven and hell. She relished the chance to gain knowledge. She shrank from being in such close proximity to a man she suspected had the power to rip her out of her cushioning cocoon of devotion to Ben. Already she had forgotten the timbre of Ben's voice. In contrast, she knew well the hushed murmur of instructions from Doctor Marshall as he hovered nearby today, directing her how to divide nerve from muscle.

Once, he touched her arm to guide the knife, and the heat of his fingers burned her skin. She felt a buzz in her body beneath the swaths of her enveloping apron.

She stopped, lifted the knife from the patient, and lied, "I cannot do this."

"You are well on your way," he protested. "See, turn the scalpel so." His firm touch on her hand assisted her movement. She fought to sweep his effect on her into a far corner so that she could finish the living lesson.

"There, that's the way. You have a natural feel for surgery."

His praise almost stung, for his voice was filled with the warmth of his approval and his regard.

She continued her work, wondering if she shook ever so slightly from anxiety or as a result of him putting his hands on both of her own in the next step. Then he released her left hand and encircled her body with his left arm to get a different angle. Now she stood trapped between his arms.

The scent of bay rum swirled up her nostrils. The heat of his torso against her back made her go still. She held her breath, felt the buzz spread and heat up her veins.

"Don't stop," he said, his breath warm on the top of her ear. "This part is crucial."

She realized his attention was wrapped up in the surgery, in the instruction. He was not intent upon inappropriate behavior toward her. She breathed again. Made the incision he directed her to do. Watched the blood pool in the cavity as he showed her how to tie off the blood vessel. His arm came away from around her, releasing her from the intimate position so he could complete the suture. Her back felt cold without him near. The buzz diminished and finally ceased.

When the surgical lesson was finished and the patient had been released to the care of several nurses, Doctor Marshall beamed at her. "Well done," he said, as he washed blood from his naked forearms in a basin. She looked away. The hair on his arms was black and thick. She couldn't remember if Ben had much hair on his arms, or what color it had been. Her fingers twitched as she waited her turn at the washing bowl. Was the black hair coarse or fine?

She winced as it came to her that she wanted to touch his bare arm to find out. Shame flooded her. Was she forgetting Ben? How could she? He it was who had wrapped his arms around her, drawn her close, made love to her. But the man standing beside her, the cheerful, confident man with flesh on his bones and dark hair on that flesh, had within the hour past held her in an approximation of an embrace, and her body had betrayed her devotion to her dead husband.

"You'll make a surgeon very soon," he said, and brushed a knuckle against her chin. She turned and thrust her hands into the bloody water in the bowl. Ben had often touched her on the chin in nearly the same way. She bit her lip to prevent tears from flooding her eyes. *I must think of Ben.*

Alex left the surgery, taking slow breaths as he strode down the corridor. *She is coming along*, he thought. Her natural instincts almost made his instruction unnecessary. Almost, but not quite. He was thankful for the "not quite" limits to her knowledge, to her skills. Acquiring more dexterity would take months.

He opened the door to his office, stepped inside, closed the door carefully, and leaned against it. He let his head hang forward, his arms remaining still and quiet at his sides. His fingers gradually closed into fists. Being so close to Ella Ruth in the surgical suite had proven difficult in controlling his feelings for her. He knew it would be hard, and he had determined to remain aloof, a teacher with his student; no more. The events of today's surgery had nearly sent him reeling beyond his abilities to maintain a clear head.

Why had be put his arm around the woman? He could have gently moved her to the side, taken the scalpel and probe and shown her how that step was accomplished, instead of guiding her hands. The position had been a mockery of an embrace, a shell of the whole act.

He brought his head up against the door and let resolve fill his bones. He must be careful in the future. He must not indulge himself in further simulations of romantic touch, however unconscious. Mrs. Benjamin Owen must be horrified at the action. He had promised her they would be instructor and student. Teacher and pupil. Master and apprentice.

He groaned.

When he had become conscious of how he had positioned himself, with her within the circle of his arms, he had almost lost concentration, almost forgotten the patient beneath their melded hands. How had he been so foolish?

"I must maintain my distance," he muttered. "She's good enough to take on the whole of a surgery. I can stand on the other side of the table."

It wasn't true. They had only begun the tutelage process. But he must never again compromise his promise to Ella Ruth. Not so long as her dead husband stood like a ghostly apparition between them.

Benjamin Owen, when will you turn her loose?

Ella Ruth pressed her hands to her abdomen after Dr. Marshall's retreat. The scent of his bay rum lingered in the room. Hot air swirled around her as the door opened and closed to his passage, heating her face, heating her body once more. She knew it was only the weather causing her temperature to rise, but it seemed as though something else, something faintly remembered, seared her skin. She touched her chin where Alex's knuckle had skimmed her face. Why had he done that?

The oppressive heat cloaking her must be abated, cooled. She longed for the days of childhood, when she was accustomed to wade in the low waters of the river bordering her father's property. Cool water had helped her pass the long summer days in relative comfort, even if it had been a tom-boy thing to do.

She tried to turn aside the thought of her youthful foolishness, but remembered the stream passing through the hospital grounds, just beyond the garden. Perhaps running water could ease her state of unrest so she could think of Ben.

She tidied up the operatory room, took the soiled linens to the laundry, and then went out through the kitchen into the garden. A white, new moon stood in the sky, a pale ghost of its nighttime appearance.

Nurse Gordon, now Matron Gordon, came toward her, carrying a bushel basket filled with roses newly clipped from bushes that stood guard on the outskirts of the kitchen part of the garden. She stopped when she had come near to Ella Ruth.

"Mrs. Owen," she said brightly. "Such a lovely day. The men do enjoy the flowers so. Sniff that big red one. Such a lovely scent." She inhaled a large portion of the odor herself and looked at Ella Ruth with a sideways glance. "The patients miss you on the ward."

"You are doing a grand job of replacing me. I would not have thought of bringing in flowers. Well done."

The woman colored, her face beaming at the praise. "They still miss you, ma'am. They speak about you praying with them."

Ella Ruth felt her body releasing the strain of the last hours. "You may tell them I think fondly of them," she said, and turned back to accompany her to Ward Three. "Let me help you with the roses. I have time enough."

She momentarily forgot her need of the stream of cooling water behind the garden, and arranged roses into containers to distribute throughout the ward until Thomas came for her.

Chapter 10

Ella Ruth spent her time in the hospital, when she was not in surgery, helping manage the closet of surgical supplies and linens, and reading the medical texts Dr. Marshall had inherited from Dr. Kellner. Dr. Marshall had moved into the Director's office, leaving his old one open for the new addition to the staff, Dr. Edward Fergen. All of her activities brought her into contact with Dr. Marshall.

One day as she sat in an armchair in the office reading a fairly new medical journal article on the need for sterile instruments, Dr. Marshall entered with a pile of mail tucked under his arm. He greeted her, then sat behind the desk to open the letters.

The windows stood open behind him, flooded with yellow sunshine. Bees buzzed on their way to a new flower.

"Huh," Dr. Marshall grunted at one point.

Ella Ruth looked up. The doctor's brows were drawn together in an indication of worry. She asked, "Distressing news?"

He put down the letter and Dr. Kellner's ornate brass opener, passed his hand over the sheet of paper as though to uncrease it, then glanced at her. "Actually, no," he said, looking back down at the missive. "It's a notice of an event." He cleared his throat, but said nothing further.

Mildly disturbed that she was curious about the event, as she had an idea it would not have anything to do with her, she went back to her reading.

Several moments later, she realized that Dr. Marshall had not continued to open his mail, and a glance in his direction told her that he sat still, holding the event notice between his two hands, gazing at her.

"Is something amiss, Doctor?"

He looked at the paper again and answered in a shaky voice, "No."

She marked her place, put the journal aside on a small table beside her, and got to her feet. "I can see that you are upset."

His reaction as she began to move toward him was to refold the paper and put it into his drawer.

"There is nothing to be done about it," he answered, his voice retaining the shakiness.

"Nonsense," she said. "All problems have a resolution of some kind." She stood before his desk, noting his pale face and a drop of sweat coursing its way off his brow.

He slowly raised his gaze from the desktop to her eyes. "There is no remedy."

"Doctor Marshall, Alexander, are you ill?" She had never used his name to his face before, but it seemed appropriate in the circumstances.

His face whitened even more. "I 'm not ill. I cannot—" His hand twitched on the desk, fetching up against the ink well. He grabbed it to steady it. "You would not . . ." His voice trailed off in misery.

"I would not what?" She wanted to lean across the

desk and touch his brow to see if, indeed, he was ill. She refrained, due to the distraught look in his eyes.

He shook his head in a slight gesture.

"Alex, you must tell me what is amiss, since I seem to be involved."

He blinked, once, twice, three times. "Ella Ruth." His gaze dropped.

"Alex, please."

There, she had used the short version of his name twice in a row, and it had not scorched her mouth. He had used her name, and instead of bringing her pain, she rather liked the sound of it coming from his lips. But his voice had been so weak. She tried again to cajole him to reveal the matter. "Please tell me."

He looked up in resignation. "The commander of the garrison invites me to an officer's ball in celebration of Independence Day. I am to bring my lady." He stopped, amended his words. "A lady to accompany me. I have no lady."

She felt sick. Independence Day for the Yankees. July Fourth.

"I cannot ask you," he said, a ghostly smile on his face. "That would be anathema to you."

"Anath— anathema?"

"A great embarrassment, a cursed trial. Against your convictions," he continued in explanation. His face had regained a bit of color. "I must go, however. One doesn't turn down an invitation from the garrison commander."

"Politics," she whispered.

He nodded.

"Will you be greatly scorned if you do not have a lady on your arm?" She didn't know why it mattered to her. She didn't want the man to suffer, though. "Will you lose your place?"

He stiffened, as though he had not thought of such a thing. At last, he answered. "I don't think so. I doubt the army commands the medical corps."

"That is good." Alex was right. She could not stomach the thought of attending a Yankee celebration, of seeing rank upon rank of Yankee officers pass before her eyes. But Alex needed a lady to accompany him. She shivered. "You could probably ask Matron Gordon to attend with you." The instant she uttered the words, she felt pierced in the bosom by the thought. "She is unencumbered," she pressed forward with the idea, hating the roiling in her stomach. *Ben!* she thought, and pain sickened her again.

Confused by her conflicted emotional responses, she said, "I think I hear Thomas coming for me," and left the room with hurried steps, feeling Alex's eyes boring into her back.

She's right. I should probably ask Matron Gordon.

Alex leaned his chair back, clasping the fingers of both hands behind his neck. The fact that Miriam Gordon held no attraction for him didn't enter into the matter. However, he wasn't partial to red-headed women. They often had unappealing dispositions.

"Alex," he told himself. "It's only one evening."

An evening of misery. What if asking her to attend

with me raises further expectations in her? That was an unsettling thought. He'd never sought a friendship with the matron, nor any other woman at the hospital. Was this the time to do otherwise?

He left the chair and began to pace, a larger circuit than had been possible in his old office. Dr. Kellner had chosen a larger room for himself, almost double the size of Alex's old domain.

His mind screamed, Ask her, ask her. It's only one night. His body answered, She's not Ella Ruth.

She was not available to attend with him. He had to get used to that idea. The woman didn't bear him any affection and, it seemed, never would. Benjamin Owen held her fast.

I have time yet to arrive at a solution, he decided, and went back to his desk to finish opening the mail.

That evening, Ella Ruth sought the solace of the garden again, wearing her dinner attire of the fine lavender-colored, lawn dress made up from the material her mother had purchased last winter. The light-weight fabric suited the warm air of the evening, not yet cooled from the descent of the sun.

"Ben," she said as she strode around the walk between the borders softly scented with the blooms of annuals. "You must help me." Moonlight softened the shadows of the trees. "I am doing fulfilling work at the hospital." She put ten fingertips to her forehead, bent her neck slightly. Stopped walking. Closed her eyes. "I adore you. I always will do so." Weakness swept over her, and she let her arms lower to her sides. "I have tried so hard to be your faithful relic. It has been my determination to remain true to your memory."

She felt a sob moving upwards in her throat. She opened her eyes and began to walk again, gazing upward at the sky. "Ben, do you remember me? Do you love me? Are you up there among the stars? Are you riding the moon?" The thought of him perched astride the moon instead of atop Blackie, his beloved horse, made her smile and beat back the sob.

"I have a new position at the hospital. Working there has given me purpose again. I'm coming to feel alive, instead of remaining the dried-up husk I've been since you . . . died. Oh Ben, am I allowed to leave off grieving and turn my attention to study, to work, to becoming a surgeon?"

Ben didn't say anything back to her, which of course, was impossible, as he was dead, long buried somewhere in a Waynesboro field. A wash of resignation went through her heart. She came up to a bench that stood in front of the pungent chaste tree with its clusters of blue blossoms and sank down upon the wooden seat.

"I wish you could answer me. I wish I could hear your voice. Nowadays I only hear the voice of the surgeon, Doctor Marshall. He is training me in medicine and surgery." She bent over, hid her face in her hands. "He finds me attractive, Ben. I don't know how that can be. I'm not a merry girl any longer. My face is too thin. My curves . . . are slight." She swallowed. "His hands are strong and sure as he guides my hands above a patient. Ben, please. I am so confused."

Ben made no reply.

She straightened up. "He needs an escort. I'm sorry, I mean he needs a companion, someone he can escort to a fancy party he must attend. He won't ask me to accompany him. He won't wound me in that way. Ben, I fear he loves me, or thinks he does. Help me know what to do."

She felt a light touch brushing her chin. She inhaled sharply, then let the breath leave her lungs slowly. It had only been a breeze moving through the garden. She was sure of it. What else could it be?

She sat very still, wondering if she was right. No breeze stirred the bushes. The four o'clock blossoms did not sway. Neither did the snapdragons. The heliotrope remained steadfastly in place.

Ben?

She felt his presence then, after months and months of nothing. His fingers stroked her neck, and she bent it sideways to accommodate his touch. Her eyes closed as a chill beat up her spine. She moaned, "I love you," and a ghostly finger stilled her lips.

He's a good man.

Her eyes came open at that thought, which was not hers. "But a Yankee," she blurted out.

A good man, came again to her mind.

Ben's phantom lips pressed hers for a fleeting moment, then he was gone and the branches of the chaste tree behind her rustled.

How Ben loved irony.

She sat alone in the moonlit garden, trying to understand. After more than a year, he had come to comfort her, and she did feel comforted. She also felt a different emotion, one that should confuse her, distress her. That it did not was what she had to understand.

"Whooooo."

Ella Ruth started, then looked upward into the boughs of the sweetgum tree across the path and heard the resident barn owl rustling its wings before it took flight. *Who?*

She rose to her feet, stiff from sitting so long on the bench in the garden. Momma must be worried that she'd been out here so long. She walked slowly back to the door, gooseflesh rising on her arms. The air remained pleasantly warm. Cool air was not an excuse for chills.

Ben came to me, she marveled.

Her feet on the stairs did not stumble as she ascended. She paused on the landing and stared down into the foyer below. Momma came out of the parlor, leaving the doorway open so that Ella Ruth heard the murmur of male voices. Poppa. Merlin.

She gave a little wave of her hand to assure her mother that all was well, then turned and went toward her bedroom.

Lula greeted her and helped her out of the new dress. As her maid carried it away to hang it, Ella Ruth donned a light nightgown and climbed into bed.

Lula came over to the bedside table and lifted the lamp. "Goodnight, Missy." She walked toward the door.

"Thank you, Lula."

Sleep did not come easily. Why had Ben come? The

question chased around her mind for what seemed like hours, but may have only been minutes, before she arrived at a conclusion. *He came to release me, to split open my cocoon.*

Chapter 11

Alex shuffled a pile of papers from his desk to the shelf behind him and sighed as he sat once more in his leather swivel chair. Doctor Kellner's erstwhile office was becoming untidy. He wished he had one-half of the organizational skills of the deposed director. Perhaps he needed a secretary to deal with the overflowing paperwork, but where would he get funds for another body in the hospital? And where would he put the man? He and Mrs. Owen already filled up the office, he at his desk, and she in the reading chair, unless she was tending to other duties he'd give her from time to time.

The matter of the Independence Day Ball still hung over his head. He had not approached Matron Gordon yet. How could he? He only had one vision for the event, and it included Mrs. Owen—Ella Ruth—try as he might to get it out of his mind.

She walked in then, moving light as an afternoon breeze to the chair, but she did not sit. Her face was hidden, so he couldn't divine the reason for her hesitation. She straightened her shoulders and turned to face him.

"I will attend the Officers' Ball with you," she said, her voice low, and yet, it had a musical intonation to it, as though some structure within her throat had changed.

He rose to his feet, surprise lifting him like an aerial observer's balloon. "I—" he said, and stopped, unable to craft a coherent response.

She walked toward his desk, her face more serene than he had ever seen it. "I may not like being in the company of so many military officers, but I will endure it for your sake." Her skin and hair glowed briefly as she passed through a ray of morning sun from the eastern window.

His tongue loosened for a moment. "For my sake."

She came to a stop before his desk, blinked a few times as she rested her fingertips on the edge of his desk, then lowered her eyes to gaze at them. "You are a good man, Doctor Marshall. If you must play politics, I can do my part to assist you."

"Assist me?"

Her chin lifted in the familiar show of spirit. "Am I not your assistant?"

"You are." He couldn't seem to breathe correctly.

"Then I shall assist you in this matter."

"Ella Ruth!" Now his breath came quickly. "You are sure? You will do this thing? For me?"

She looked around the room, her eyes beginning to widen as though she were rethinking her generous offer. He willed one foot, then another, to move him from behind the desk, to circle it so he could stand closer to her and perhaps prevent a precipitous escape.

He didn't dare reach out a hand to touch her. The moment was too fragile, too fraught with possibilities, and he couldn't shatter it with a wrong movement, a badly executed action. Instead, he stared at her, into the depths of her cornflower blue eyes, and stood as still as the iron dog-shaped door stop resting against the wall.

The panic had left her eyes, left them soft and gentle and—

He pressed a fisted hand into the cup of the other and felt the muscles of his arms strain.

Accepting.

Acceptance had never been in her eyes before. Always, there had been a wariness, a caution, a protective, defensive light. Now her eyes were soft. Yes. Gentle. Yes. Accepting.

Yes.

She blinked, shook her head by a fraction of an inch. "My parents will encourage me."

He held back a frown, thinking it would startle her. What did her parents have to do with her decision? Then he remembered that they wanted to normalize their status. Had Ella Ruth spoken to them? Had they persuaded her to take this action?

No. Her eyes did not hold a hint of resentment. She had come to this decision herself.

"Mrs. Owen, I am honored that you have—" He stumbled over his words, then continued. "That you will accompany me to the Officer's Ball." He let the formality hang in the air, in case she wanted to say something further.

She smiled. The simple, slight movement of her lips and cheeks changed her aspect, and he nearly sucked in his breath at the beauty of it. He restrained himself, savoring the sight of the delicate creases at the sides of her mouth, the pink tinge of her cheeks, the light in her eyes. He couldn't ask her if she knew how glorious she was. Not now. Perhaps a time would come . . .

His eyes widened at the audacity of his thought. He hastily followed it up with an almost curt, "I will collect you at six o'clock."

She nodded. "Thomas will accompany us."

Thomas?

"That is, our butler will ride behind." She put her hand to her collar, pressing it against her neck. "What is the expected dress?"

He thought for a moment. "As formal as you can arrange for," he said at last. In view of the fact that times were still hard in Virginia, he knew he could not expect to see her attired in a ball gown. "In deference to your feelings, I will wear civilian clothing instead of my uniform. I believe I can manage to get away with that."

Her eyes softened. "I will see what Mother can devise," she said, and strode out of the room.

"Oh my word," Ella Ruth whispered to herself as she made her exit from Dr. Marshall's office. One hand covered her bosom, feeling the thunder galloping through her heart. Why had she committed to attending the Ball with him? She pondered the answer as she went into the surgery to lay out the instruments and materials the doctor and she would need for the operation to be performed later in the morning.

She knew she was shaking in the aftermath of her declaration of support. Was that what it was? Simply a supportive action to keep him from having to attend the affair alone?

Was she lying to herself? How many years had it

been since she had attended a dancing party? She wondered if she remembered the order of steps in a reel, a quadrille? Would there be a grand march to begin the festivities? Could she march abreast down a long hall with Yankee officers and their ladies?

She thought of Alex. He needed to attend and was expected to have a lady on his arm. She didn't want it to be Matron Gordon.

Her hand stilled, clutching a steel probe. Where had that thought come from? She had proposed the idea, after all. Had Alex already asked the tall, comely matron to be his guest? Had she misspoken in his office?

But the fact remained. She *didn't* want Alex to collect Miriam Gordon and walk into the ballroom with her on his arm.

A fierce squeezing sensation strangled her lungs for a moment. She put down the probe and went to the basin across the room. She poured water from a pitcher into the vessel. She dipped her hands in the liquid, then stroked her forehead with one wet hand. Why was her face warm?

"I can't be jealous," she told herself in a firm but quiet tone. She pushed away the emotion. Alex had said he would collect *her*, Ella Ruth Allen, for the Ball. If she had caused him a quandary, she must let him sort it out.

Something was awry in her past thought, but she couldn't discover what it was. No matter. She was going to a Ball, and she was determined to have a good time.

~*~*~

Alex stared after Ella Ruth as she departed. He was

left breathless in the wake of her decision to attend the Ball with him. Her declaration saved him from having to approach Matron Gordon. That was a relief.

He waited for a moment more, then tried to inhale. The breath came hard to him, and was shaky and brought in scant air, but he was relieved anew to learn that he hadn't forgotten how to perform the function so necessary to life.

He looked around at the office. What was it that he had to do today? He caught sight of a paper Ella Ruth had placed on his desk yesterday before she left for the day. Today's schedule. A surgery at ten o'clock. Ah. He would continue his role of teacher. This time, he would be very careful how he approached his instruction, as he did not want a repeat of the last unconscious mimicry of an embrace. That had been unfair to them both, and had shaken him more than he wanted to admit.

Well, this time, he would be cautious. He would have Ella Ruth step aside while he showed her the art of the surgeon. Would she learn sufficiently if he did not guide her hands? Did not take the instruments herself? It would have to do. He dared not risk a repetition, for his own sanity.

Momma was beside herself when Ella Ruth informed her of the news.

"You have nothing to wear!"

No, she didn't. The delicate lawn dress, although nearly new, was not elegant enough to count as a ball gown. Ella Ruth had worn through practically every article of clothing she still possessed. She had grown taller since the giddy girlhood days when satin dresses and silken finery seemed to be the most important things in the world to her. Years of the privations of war had intervened, had forced her to grow up, to change her immature and frivolous ways of thinking.

She patted the slice of broomstick under her dress. She couldn't wear it to the Ball. It didn't make a very pretty decoration for a formal event. She would have to lay it aside for the night.

Momma came into Ella Ruth's bedroom, carrying a large bundle almost as long as she was tall, which was wrapped in an abundance of white cloth. The bundle smelled of lavender and other herbs.

"I found this in a trunk in the attic," Momma said. "I had forgotten I still had this gown. Perhaps it will serve, with a little creative alteration."

She laid the bundle across the bed and began to peel aside the protective cloth covering. As she did so, pale gold satin shimmered in the rays of the late afternoon sunlight pouring through Ella Ruth's bedroom windows. She remembered this gown from her childhood. Momma had worn it to an important ball in Harrisburg to which the governor had come. That had been an exciting night. Ella Ruth had begged to be included in the festivities, to be allowed to wear her own prettiest dress to the ball, but her mother had put her off. "One day you shall wear this gown to your own ball. All in good time, Daughter."

Ella Ruth shivered involuntarily. How the world had changed in the intervening years. She stroked the soft fabric, recalling her frivolous dreams. She had not had occasion to wear Momma's golden gown up to now. How ironic that she was to wear it to an officer's ball held by the occupation army's garrison.

"Satin is warm for summer," Momma murmured. "Perhaps if we shorten the sleeves? Have you any long gloves, Ella Ruth?"

"G-g-gloves?" she scoffed. "Neither short nor long, Momma."

"Be that as it may, you will glow exceedingly if you do not have enough air circulating about you. Bare arms must do." She turned to another problem. "If I recall, the bodice is quite impossibly low. I almost couldn't bear to wear it, but your father insisted. The women were scandalized, but the men, including your father, seemed to enjoy the spectacle." Momma raised one eyebrow. "You are more slender of build than I. The bodice will come down even lower on you. There is a piece of lace in the trunk. I believe it is enough to fill in the bodice. I'll think about what trim we can put around shorter sleeves. Perhaps . . ."

As Momma made her mental calculations, Ella Ruth removed her bodice and skirt, forgetting that this exposed the token of her marriage to view. She hastily lifted the gown over her head and let it slip down over her arms to cover her underclothing. *Oh my!* The bodice fell far too low, even allowing for future alterations of breadth to accommodate her slender form.

Her mother turned, caught sight of the piece of broomstick laying against Ella Ruth's skin, and said in a strained voice, "I believe I have a necklace and earrings that will suit the occasion much better."

Ella Ruth covered the memento with her hand. "Thank you, Momma. I will not wear this to the Ball." She fingered the wood.

"That is well. The good doctor may not understand the significance of your rough ornament."

"No, Alex knows nothing of it." She lowered her hand and the soft satin slid down her arm to cover her fingers.

"Alex? Is that Doctor Marshall's name?"

Horrified at her mistake, Ella Ruth turned to stare out the window until she could formulate a response. The sheer curtain across the window was trimmed with lace. She strode across the room and touched it.

"Will this serve to trim the sleeves, Momma?" She turned back. Her mother had a hand to her mouth, trying to mask a smile.

"Do you call him Alex at the hospital?" Momma's voice was muffled by her hand.

"That wouldn't be proper."

"Have you done so?" Momma's hand lowered, and she tittered before she spoke again. "Not proper at all. When did you begin to think of him in familiar terms?"

"I don't," she said slowly, confused by a swirl of emotion that belied her words.

"Oh, darling girl." Momma came and swept her into an embrace. She kissed her temple. "Are you forming an attachment to Doctor Marshall?"

"I must not," Ella Ruth said, her voice strangled. "I am Benjamin Owen's relic." Then she remembered the thoughts Ben had planted in her mind in the garden, and the unnamed emotion that followed. It was very like the one she felt now. She recalled the twinges of jealousy she had experienced when she thought of Alex taking Miriam to the Ball in her place. "Oh Momma. Perhaps I am."

"That would not be the worst thing to befall you." Momma patted her on the back. "You've already lived through a calamitous war and survived it. You've lost your lover—I mean, your husband—to death. It may be time to accept—" Momma sniffed and seemed to struggle to continue. "My dear little Ella," she said through thick emotion. "You have become so strong."

"Momma." Ella Ruth twisted in her mother's arms. "Please don't dampen the satin." She knew it sounded harsh and petty, but tears would stain the fabric to a ruin. She shrugged out of the encircling arms, hastily pulled off the gown, threw it onto the bed, and then went back to her mother to comfort her. Her arms slid about her. "You and Poppa have been so patient with me. Thank you for your kindness."

Momma began to sob.

"You have endured much at my hand. Forgive my selfishness through the years."

Momma still cried.

Ella Ruth squeezed her mother, then, after long minutes, tried another tack to divert her from tears. "I haven't a hoop for the gown."

Momma sniffed and wiped her nose with a bit of common muslin. "I think hoop skirts are out of fashion now," she whispered, then blew her nose.

Ella Ruth giggled. "We can use the rest of the sheer curtain for an adornment of some sort at the back of the dress. I believe that will help."

"That is a brilliant thought, Daughter. I shall see what I can do."

Ella Ruth furrowed her brow. "Can we afford the services of a dressmaker?"

"I was accounted quite a fair hand with a needle and shears in my day." Momma's tears were forgotten. "In fact, I designed and sewed many of my dresses in my youth. My mother took delight in my skills."

"You surprise me, Momma."

"I wasn't always a pampered wife." Momma chuckled. "I used my talents to secure the attentions of a man who was well on his way to becoming wealthy."

Ella Ruth wanted to know the truth of what she had long suspected. "It wasn't a love match."

Momma's gaze slid sideways, then returned. "We have become quite fond of each other through the years."

Ella Ruth stood very still. Was it unfair that she herself had garnered the admiration and love of one man, and now another seemed devoted to her? Warmth spread up her neck as her bosom filled with yearning. Her thoughts flashed to Ben, then shifted to center upon Alex. No. Not unfair at all.

Chapter 12

Ella Ruth stared into the wavy old cheval mirror supported by a cherry wood frame in Momma's bedroom. She could scarcely believe the miracles her mother had wrought with the satin gown and a few odds and ends of lace and sheer curtain material. She ran one hand down her flat stomach, ending at the row of white lace that came together to a point at the front. She fingered it. What would Alex think of the gown? Of how she looked in it?

"The gown is beautiful, Momma! How did you manage such marvelous work?"

Momma's eyes held unspilled tears. "You look beautiful in it, my dear." Her voice sounded thick. "I trust you will make a fine impression tonight."

I hope so. I hope Alex will like how I look. "I will try."

"Oh. I nearly forgot." Momma went to her chest of drawers and opened the thin top drawer. She picked out a small bundle that looked like cotton and brought it over to Ella Ruth. She spread the top of the bundle apart with one hand, then picked up a sparkling necklace. "Hold it for me," she said, and when Ella Ruth took it in shaking fingers, Momma shook a pair of earrings into her free hand.

"The Antwerp diamonds." Ella Ruth's voice came out small and hushed. She had only seen them once before, long before the war.

"I buried them beneath the potting shed," Momma said.

Ella Ruth thought of all the time she had spent with Ben in that shed, keeping him away from the Yankees while he healed, until it was safe to take him into the house. It didn't matter. If she had dug them up, she couldn't have done anything with them at the time, couldn't have kept them safe.

Momma placed the puffy cotton swathing on the bed and started to insert the earrings into the small holes in Ella Ruth's ear lobes. She frowned. "You have not worn earrings for too long a time. The holes are nearly closed."

Ella Ruth sighed. "Push the posts through, Momma. It won't hurt much."

The actions hurt more than she wanted to admit, but once Momma had finished putting on the earring backs and had fastened the necklace around her throat, Ella Ruth could hardly breathe at the spectacular view in the old mirror. She had not looked like this in a very long time. In truth, she probably had never looked like this: eyes sparkling to rival the diamonds, cheeks tinged pink with excitement, wearing a glorious dress that complemented her coloring much better . . . yes, far better than did the black she had worn for so many months.

To honor Ben.

To keep his memory alive in her sorrowing heart.

To show her devotion as a proper relic must.

But Ben had come to the garden and released her

from her increasingly lonely state. *He's a good man.* Only four words and a few ghostly caresses to comfort and assure her, and then he was gone, back to riding the moon, or whatever spirits did in an afterlife she had never given thought to.

Momma's sniff behind her brought her back to the sight in the looking glass. She hoped her appearance would honor Alex, give him comfort as he did his duty in attending the Ball.

Her breath came faster as Momma murmured, "Beautiful! You will make an indelible impression, Daughter."

She was going to a Ball, a magnificent dancing party, a pleasure robbed from her youth by the War. She hoped Alex would approve her looks, the dress, her willingness to attend. She hoped the slight pain in her earlobes would recede as she made the friendly gesture for the man she . . . appreciated.

Her heart raced. She didn't dare name the true emotion that squeezed her bosom. How long before Alex arrived?

"What is the time, Momma?"

"The time?" She looked at the mantel clock. "It's a quarter hour to six." She moved to a table near the door and brought back a small plate upon which a half-slice of buttered brown bread lay. "You must eat this, Ella, to keep your stomach calm."

Ella Ruth snatched the bread, knowing a protestation was futile. Leaning over to keep crumbs from falling onto the gold satin, she took a large, quick bite, chewed it as rapidly as though she were in some sort of race, then swallowed to clear her mouth.

"Eat it all, my dear."

Three more bites chewed and gulped down in quick succession did the job. Momma handed her a napkin, and she patted her mouth to remove any residue.

"I think a little color on your lips is in order," Momma said, and handed her a small glass jar of lip pomade.

Ella Ruth opened the jar and went to the mirror. There wasn't much of the color left in the bottom of the jar. Momma must have hoarded it throughout the years of difficulty. She touched the pomade tentatively. It was waxy and a bit hard, but softened under her finger sufficiently that she could retrieve a tiny amount on the tip on her finger. She leaned close to the looking glass's surface, and carefully daubed the color onto the curvature of her lips. It went on smoothly, accenting the sensitive skin with a soft red hue.

When she had finished applying the pomade, Momma came up with the napkin and rubbed it over her fingertip. A slight stain remained.

"The color will stay on your lips for hours," Momma whispered. "Your father brought me the jar from Paris after one of his business trips abroad. The color." She stopped, a faint pink rising into her cheeks. "The color excited his ardor," she finished in a husky voice.

"Oh Momma. You mustn't talk—"

"Men are influenced by the oddest circumstances." She took the jar from Ella Ruth and returned it to her dressing table. "Make the most of that with your Alex."

Ella Ruth shrank from the thought of using

contrived behavior in her budding relationship, but the breathless state of her bosom spoke of excitement and anticipation. She would use no coquettishness on Alex as she had on Ben. There was no need to be coy. The man already . . . had an attraction to her, an affection for her. She stopped short of attributing any deeper emotion to him as the doorbell chimed.

Momma patted her arm. "You look splendid."

Alex stood on the stoop, waiting for the great brown door to open. When it did, he looked down into the dark eyes of the butler, Thomas.

"I am here for Miss Ella Ruth," he said to the servant, feeling somewhat foolish to be announcing what was clearly his purpose.

"Yes sir, I know that. Come in, please. I'll see if she is ready for your party."

Alex stepped into the foyer. As the butler retreated and slowly climbed the wide, curved staircase to the upper floor, Alex wondered if Ella Ruth was truly ready to accompany him to a "Yankee" event. He waited for several long minutes, staring at the spot where he imagined she would appear, his stomach clenching with anxiety. Could she possibly enjoy the evening? She had made it very clear that she was accompanying him to prevent him from being shamed. She had said nothing of excitement or eager anticipation.

Then she was there, standing at the top of the staircase, encompassed in golden light, it seemed, as the fabric of her gown shimmered and gleamed in the light of the candle sconces on the landing. A necklace of what looked to be diamonds, along with diamond studs adorning her earlobes, added light to the portrait.

His breath left his body in a whoosh. Her golden hair was drawn back from her astonishingly beautiful face, and looked like it tumbled softly down her back. He couldn't be sure of that yet, but it wasn't piled high on her head. Her cheeks looked a bit flushed, but that could be from excitement, after all.

She placed her bare hand on the bannister and started down the stairs, toward him. She neither smiled nor frowned, but her aspect was pleasant, so she must be having some enjoyment. He watched her take each step lower, and as she descended, her lips—tinted a glowing red—lifted into a genuine smile.

Then she stood on the last stair, at a level to gaze directly into his eyes, and his heart swelled with pride in her, of her looks, to be sure, but more fully of her generous soul and willingness to do him a great favor.

"Alex," she murmured, her voice husky.

"Miss Ella Ruth," he answered. He wanted more than life to take her in his arms and kiss those sweet red lips, but he held himself back, frightened at the intensity of his desire to flaunt convention and claim her in her parents' foyer.

Her eyes went wide as she evidently recognized his strong emotion. "We must be off," she said, her voice strong enough to carry to the landing as she looked toward it. He looked up in turn. Her mother stood there, accompanied by a man he knew must be her father. "Goodnight, Momma, Poppa," she said, then accepted a short wrap from her maid, who had come into the foyer from a side door. "Thank you, Lula." She carried the wrap over her arm instead of putting it on in the summer warmth. It was for later, when the heat of the day had left the night cool.

Thomas, who must have used a back staircase, came through the same door that Lula had used. Another door opened, and a young man stood in the doorway, smoking a pipe and looking at them.

Alex inhaled the musky scent of the tobacco with his next breath. The young man must be her brother, the university student Merlin.

Ella Ruth confirmed his supposition when she turned toward the young man and bid him goodnight.

"Have a pleasant evening," he replied, then turned back to his parlor lair and shut the door.

Alex offered his arm to Ella Ruth, who took it and smiled at him. His heart gave a jolt in reaction as Thomas opened the front door, and then bowed them through it.

By the time they arrived at the hired buggy, Alex's heart had resumed a steady, albeit quick, pace. He handed the girl in, strode around the horse, pausing a second to let it sniff his hand, and then stepped up into the vehicle himself.

Alex clicked his tongue at the horse and flipped the lines on its rump. It started off, pulling the buggy into a jerky progress down the lane. He heard the hooves of old Thomas's horse clip-clopping behind them as the servant followed, preserving the social mandate that he and Ella Ruth be chaperoned on their journey.

He looked sideways at the wondrous girl. She sat easily on the seat beside him, hands clasped atop the wrap Lula had given her. Her hair indeed cascaded down her back in a golden torrent. The satin gown, trimmed with lace from what treasure trove he knew not, left her skin bare beneath sleeves that came midway down her upper arms. She wore no gloves, which he remembered was the style for formal ladies' wear. Where would she get long kid gloves in impoverished Virginia? No matter. She set a style all her own.

He glanced at her face. Her mouth still curved in a smile, which made the corners of his own mouth lift. A warm feeling of calm flooded his chest. This promised to be a happy occasion.

"I've never been to an officers' ball," she blurted out, surprising him at the intensity of her statement. "Will it be grand?"

He thought back to the one time he had attended such an event, and smiled, even as he remembered that the lady on his arm had been Cassie. He let the bittersweet memory slide away, concentrating on recalling the overall ambiance of that ball.

"Indeed, it will be grand. It will begin with a Grand March, a promenade to show off all the finery of both ladies and officers." He looked down at his black suit, worn intentionally to spare her feelings, and almost wished he wore instead his best uniform, complete with ribbons and geegawgery.

Ella Ruth's excitement showed in the animation

lighting her face. "I believe I can bear that. Will there be many lights? Candles aglow along the walls?"

"I haven't been to the garrison hall, but surely they will spare no expense for such a great occasion. They may even have a fireworks display."

"Fireworks?" Her lips trembled.

He hesitated before speaking. "I'm sure it will not sound like cannon fire," he said as gently as he could.

"You will be there to comfort me." Her positive statement came low and soft from her lips, and he felt his chest expand at the sound of it.

"I will." He would do everything in his power to protect her from harm, be it physical or emotional. *Nothing would please me more than to always have that task.* He couldn't tell her that, but he could comfort himself with the soon-to-be-fulfilled vision of having her on his arm this night. He must not hope for more than that.

Ella Ruth could not stop herself from chattering about the Ball as the horse drew the buggy onward down the street, until it turned into the path which led toward the garrison post. Then an attack of nerves silenced her. She felt Alex's eyes on her. He must sense her apprehension.

"You don't need to go," he said. "If you'd rather not—"

"Momma would be mortified if I didn't attend," she whispered. She glanced in his direction, although she didn't meet his eyes before she faced forward again. "I

would be mortified at going back on my promise to you."
She flicked her eyes again in his direction and found
herself gazing into his deep brown eyes. "You are a
Yankee officer, yet you are an honorable man. I know
that now." She paused and ran the tip of her tongue over
her lips. She tasted the slightly bitter residue of the
pomade. *I must not keep licking my lips, or the pomade
will not last.* "If you are honorable, there must be other
Yankee officers of valor. Perhaps one or two of them will
be in attendance."

Alex smiled hugely. "I'm sure you are right. I can't
believe you will be ill-treated by anyone. However—" He
took her hand and squeezed it. "I will be there at your
side throughout the affair."

She could not keep back a sigh of relief. This man
who cared for her would *take care* of her tonight. She
had nothing to fear. Even when Alex did not release her
hand right away, she knew he would treat her kindly and
be her protector.

She felt the apprehension leave and squeezed his
hand. He looked startled to realize that he still held hers,
and let it go, pulling hard on the lines as they reached
their destination.

"Do have an enjoyable time," he said quietly. "If you
do not wish to dance with any Yankee who asks, only
make it known to me, and I will step in."

"Oh! I hadn't even thought of that possibility," she
said, looking down at the hands in her lap. "Thank you. I
imagine I shall not need your assistance in such a
circumstance. I am unknown."

"But very beautiful," he muttered, almost beneath

her hearing.

She felt a stab of pleasure. She had made a favorable impression tonight on Dr. Alexander Marshall.

Chapter 13

Alex found a place to park the buggy. He signaled Thomas to deal with the horse, then helped Ella Ruth down from the vehicle. She glowed with excitement, her eyes clear and bright. He offered his arm, and she took hold of it with a smile. He basked in the joy of that smile, feeling a bubbling rise of it in his own chest.

The double doors to the garrison hall stood open, spilling light and the sound of many voices into the soft evening air. Ella Ruth hesitated for a split second, then strode forward, clutching his arm as though she would never turn it loose. Then they were inside, enwrapped in gaiety and a strong aura of celebration.

He glanced down and caught Ella Ruth looking up at him, trepidation casting shadows into her eyes. "You are safe," he said, and patted her arm.

In return, she tightened her grip on his elbow, blinked several times, and gave her head a slight shake.

He bent to whisper assurances in her ear, repeating that she was safe with him. She made a small sound that seemed born of both gratitude and terror, then swallowed hard and whispered, "Thank you for your care."

His heart swelled with tenderness as they strolled down the length of the hall glittering with lamplight. Didn't she know yet how much he did care? *I haven't formally declared myself,* he recalled. He *had* mentioned his affection for her on that day when he had offered her the place as his assistant, or rather, as the operatory matron. He wondered why only days ago she had changed her mind and made her own offer to accompany him here. Something in her changed that day. Her entire attitude toward him had softened.

"Captain Marshall."

They had reached the end of the hall, where the garrison commander, Major Quentin Foote, stood with his wife at his side. The major twitched his handlebar moustache as he took in the sight of Ella Ruth. "And who do we have here?" he asked, sucking in his portly stomach.

"Major Foote, Mrs. Foote. May I present Mrs. Benjamin Owen of the City? The Widow Owen, that is," he hastened to add at the disapproving glance from Mrs. Foote. "Mrs. Owen is a matron in the hospital. She graciously agreed to act as my lady this evening."

"Ah, my very great pleasure," Major Foote said, bending over Ella Ruth's hand to bestow a kiss upon it. Alex almost laughed when Ella Ruth snatched it back, influenced, no doubt, by the glare Mrs. Foote directed at her husband.

"It is my honor to be here," Ella Ruth gushed at Mrs. Foote, who gave her a single nod.

Alex grinned on hearing the exaggerated Southern drawl in Ella Ruth's voice. *Putting the Yankees in their place.*

"We'll begin, ah, with the Grand March in a few moments," the Major said, looking at his wife. "Mrs. Foote, be so kind as to give the Captain and his lady their placement in the Order of March."

Looking like butter wouldn't melt in her mouth, Mrs. Foote said, "You and Mrs. Owen will bring up the rear, Captain Marshall. That is suitable to your position as Hospital Director." She bobbed her head, vastly pleased with herself. "It's not as though you were a *real* Army officer." Her eyes surveyed him head to foot and back again. "And out of uniform, it seems."

Evidently surprised at his wife's statement, the Major turned to her to protest. "My dear, he *is* a commissioned officer."

The lady smiled serenely. "And not stationed on the garrison post."

That was that.

Alex didn't mind bringing up the rear, and he suspected Ella Ruth had no objection, either. When the call for attention rang out in the barking voice of the Sergeant Major in attendance, he drew himself to his full height and stood still through the announcement to form up for the Grand March. Then he linked arms with Ella Ruth and moved to their place at the end of the line of officers and ladies.

The garrison band assembled at the head of the hall and tuned their instruments. Ella Ruth squirmed beside Alex, uneasy that she would not remember how to keep up with the elegant officers and their ladies. The sergeant major—present to make the announcements, she presumed—bid that fawning man, Major Foote, to lead out the Grand March with his lady.

The Major and his wife headed for the back of the hall, Mrs. Foote grasping the Major's right arm, and they came to a halt to one side of the middle of the floor and facing away from the band. Then the sergeant major called, "Choose your partners!"

Ella Ruth was pleased that she already clasped the arm of hers, as a mad scramble ensued among the younger officers for the hands of the daughters of the older officers.

"Forrrrrrrrrrrrm up," barked the sergeant major. Partners fell into line behind the Major, according to their rank, she supposed. Alex led her to the end of the row.

Then the band began to play a bright tune, sedate enough for a march but sprightly enough that it would keep the couples moving. The major made a turn to face the band, with Mrs. Foote acting as a pivot, and they started the march down the center of the hall. Ella Ruth could barely contain her excitement as the head couple approached and she and Alex moved up behind the couple ahead of them.

Don't let me stumble, she prayed, keeping step to the music.

She swiveled her head in time to see the Major and Mrs. Foote falling into line behind them as the couple who had been following them marched up the opposite, third section of the hall. Each lady gave a brief, dipping curtsy to the band as they turned. The order continued as before, and soon it was their turn to pivot and march down the middle of the hall.

Her heart beat to the rhythm of the music,

thumping hard against the wall of her bosom. She wondered if it were so loud that Alex could hear it. She glanced his way, saw his solemn countenance, and almost made a misstep. He appeared so intent on marching precisely in time to the music, that she knew he was giving her little attention at the moment. She relaxed just in time to make her curtsy as she pivoted around Alex and continued up the side of the hall.

Then, they approached the head of the line again and she turned, grasped the extended arm of a junior officer, and marched in concert with Alex, the officer, and his partner, down the length of the hall again. In front of the band, she and Alex, along with the other couple, pivoted and continued marching back to the end of the hall.

The music stirred her soul, and she began to forget any fears in the waves of exhilaration sweeping through the hall. Alex seemed to have relaxed as well, as he glanced down at her, a huge grin on his face.

Some of the couples wheeled awkwardly, but Ella Ruth soon learned the trick: the outside person stepped quickly around the half-circle turn, while the inside person marched in place, just turning his body enough to swing the rest of the line into position. She took tiny steps next to Alex, and did very well.

And just like that, they were eight people across, arms linked and stepping lightly down the hall. The music ended exactly as Major and Mrs. Foote reached the head of the hall and stopped. Each line behind then stopped in time so as not to bump into the line before them. Thus, the Grand March came to a conclusion.

Alex guided her to the side of the dance floor, whispering that Major and Mrs. Foote would begin the dancing. Her toes tapped to the time as the band began playing a tune for a new dance that was unfamiliar to her. She watched the major and his wife doing a heel-and-toe step for four beats, then sliding sideways for another four. "It's the polka dance," Alex whispered. "I'm not very good at doing it."

She felt like giggling. "I've never seen it performed before, so you're my master."

"I'll do my best," he said, squeezing the hand he still held.

Once other couples had begun to join the dance, Alex led her onto the floor, put out his arms, and she placed her hands as she had seen other ladies do. The position felt awkward at first, but as she began to move in Alex's arms to execute the steps of the dance, it became a necessity in order not to stumble or collapse. Alex held her firmly, and they managed to last through to the end of the dance without making a fatal mistake.

She sank into a chair at the side of the room and waved her hand in front of her face. "I wish I had a fan. I must have looked like a simpleton."

"No, indeed," Alex replied, taking the chair next to hers. "That was my role. You glide supremely well."

"And you overestimate my skill."

He laughed.

She spied Major Foote parting the crowd, bearing down upon her. "Quick," she said. "Ask me to dance."

Alex jumped to his feet and bowed over her upraised hand. "May I have the honor of this dance?"

"Of course." She rose and urged him toward the dance floor as Major Foote, disappointment clouding his face, arrived at her empty chair.

The dance was a waltz, another relatively new one, but Ella Ruth *did* know the steps. Alex slid them into position on the far side of the floor, took her into his arms, and executed a dipping, gliding maneuver. Ella Ruth followed him in the step, exhilarated by the narrow escape as much as by the thrill of moving so well with Alex.

From there, the night became akin to a game of hide-and-go-seek, avoiding the Major, as well as other officers who wanted to make a better acquaintance of her. She and Alex danced each figure together until the band stopped playing and the sergeant major announced a break in order to allow the participants to partake of refreshments.

They walked slowly toward the area set aside for slices of cake and a punch drink.

"You have a good grasp of the dances," Alex bent down to tell her.

"That may be so, but that last dance was more exercise than I expected."

A look of concern filled his eyes. "Are you too warm? Would you like to go outside for a breath of air?"

Ella Ruth stopped walking. She very much needed to cool her flushed face and body, but wondered how she would act when they were alone. She didn't want to alarm the man she knew she had come to esteem and appreciate with sudden protestations of affection. And yet . . . Ben had broken open her tightly-guarded emotional cocoon, had as much as told her she was free to form a new and lasting bond with whomever she chose. No, with *this* good man. Ben had been specific in the direction of his praise.

She placed her hand on his sleeve. "Yes. I would like that." She watched his eyes change color from a deep brown to almost black. He stared at her for a moment, then started toward the head of the hall and the outside door.

"I hope we won't be missed."

Ella Ruth moved toward the door as though she were in a dream. Alex held her hand tucked into the crook of his elbow, gently guiding her through the throng of couples gathered around a table holding a large punch bowl and many glass cups. When they had achieved their goal, Alex loosed her hand, and she felt as though he had abandoned her.

She knew it wasn't so, but she missed the proprietary intimacy, the feeling once again of being cherished. Then he put his hand on the small of her back, above the adornment her mother had crafted from the sheer bedroom curtain. She resisted the tendency to jerk away, then settled down and let him direct her steps away from the hall, on a path toward the moon glowing above them through gaps in the trees.

They stopped in an open area, not a garden, but a place containing a strip of lawn bordered by hedges. Beyond, bare earth stretched away toward a stand of trees.

"The parade ground," Alex explained, gesturing to the bare ground.

"Oh," she said.

Alex dropped his hand from her back. She instantly felt bereft.

He turned to face her. "Are you getting enough air?"

The area was receiving a slight breeze. "It's pleasant here," she replied.

"I am enjoying this night," he said.

She dropped her gaze. "As am I."

"I am enjoying being here with you." He paused. "I am glad I wasn't obliged to ask Matron Gordon for a favor."

She felt her heart beginning to thump wildly. "As am I," she whispered, watching the toe of Alex's right foot rise and fall in a tapping rhythm.

Neither of them said anything for a long stretch of time. Alex's foot beat time to the rhythm of Ella Ruth's heart. She thought it strange that the rhythms were exact. She saw his hand rise, felt it cup her cheek. She nestled against it, as naturally as though she had done so for years.

"I adore you," she heard him say. A bubble of joy escaped her throat as a purring moan.

"Alex," she said next, softly. He lowered his hand, but she caught it and raised it back to her cheek.

"I am forming an affection for you," she murmured, touching his sleeve below the shoulder.

"An affection? I sensed a change in you."

"Do you believe in ghosts?"

"Possibly."

She glanced at the moon. "Do you believe in the magic of moonlight?"

"I do." His voice sounded husky.

"Can it heal a heart?"

His hand trembled on her cheek. "What are you telling me?"

"Ben's ghost came to me in the garden, in the moonlight. He said you are a good man." She breathed deeply. "I had come to know that for myself, but Ben reminded me."

"Ella," he groaned, moving his face closer to hers.

She pushed softly against his shoulder so he would look at her. "Have you loved someone before?"

"I thought I did. She died of fever. I wasn't there to save her."

"Oh, Alex." She felt a surge of sympathy. "Has your heart healed?"

He didn't say anything for a long time. Just cupped her cheek with his eyes closed. "Yes," he said finally.

"I loved Ben with my whole heart. I had to learn how to give my love unselfishly, but Ben was an excellent teacher. When he died, my heart broke. I thought I would die, as well." She bowed her head again. "But I didn't. I wished to die, but death avoided me."

He took hold of her chin and raised it.

"Momma forced me to go to the hospital." She chuckled. "She didn't expect me to come home with a position, with a job of work to do. I began to live again, under your influence."

"No. You did that all on your own."

"I did not want to let another man into my heart, but—" She shrugged her shoulders. "Affection must be infectious."

He repeated his earlier question, gazing deep into her eyes. "What are you telling me?"

"Alex. Dear Alex. Ben released me to love you."

"And do you love me?" His voice was huskier than before as he brought her back to the point.

"Yes."

His hand slipped down to encircle her neck and he drew her close. He nuzzled her opposite cheek. A light streaked into the sky as a boom echoed from the far edge of the parade ground. Then a starburst opened in the sky with another loud boom.

She jumped slightly in reaction.

"The fireworks display," he murmured in her ear.

She felt her heart racing, but not from alarm.

Alex's lips moved against her cheek. "Will you do me the honor . . ."

Ella Ruth felt him swallow.

"Will you be my bride?"

A spasm of joy closed her throat for just a moment, then it released. "Yes. With all my heart," she answered.

"Your father?"

"Tomorrow," she whispered, then his mouth sought hers. She gave it freely.

Chapter 14

They married on a Sunday in August, standing before a minister in her father's parlor, with her father and mother and her brother Merlin standing behind them. Several members of the hospital staff took the roles of friends. Ella Ruth wore her almost-new lawn dress, and at her request, Alex wore his uniform. Matron Gordon had brought late roses from the hospital garden for her bouquet. Alex bore a red one in his buttonhole.

Alex and Ella Ruth made their vows in joyous, if shaky tones. The minister did his job, pronouncing them man and wife. Their kiss was chaste, but with promise for more to come.

Ella Ruth didn't want a party, so she and Alex left immediately, over her mother's strenuous objection. She didn't care. Ben had given her a second chance, the chance to love another good man. With a full heart, she got into a carriage and rode away, waving to her family and friends. Then she turned to her new family, the man who loved her as much or more than Ben had done.

"I am complete," she said. "I am whole."

Alex leaned over and nipped her ear, despite the fact that they were driving down a public street. "You were mended by moonlight."

"And by you."

The End

ABOUT THE AUTHOR

Marsha Ward writes authentic historical fiction set in 19th Century America, and contemporary romance. She was born in the sleepy little town of Phoenix, Arizona, in a simpler time. With plenty of room to roam among the chickens and citrus trees, Marsha enjoyed playing with neighborhood chums, but always had her imaginary friend, cowboy Johnny Rigger Prescott, at her side. Now she makes her home in a forest in the mountains of Arizona. She loves to hear from her readers.

Connect with her at www.marshaward.com

www.ingramcontent.com/pod-product-compliance
Lightning Source LLC
Chambersburg PA
CBHW030612130626
46552CB00002B/524